THE
DOOR
OF
NO
RETURN

THE
DOOR
OF
NO
RETURN

KWAME ALEXANDER

ANDERSEN PRESS

This edition first published in 2023 by
Andersen Press Limited
20 Vauxhall Bridge Road, London SW1V 2SA, UK
Vijverlaan 48, 3062 HL Rotterdam, Nederland
www.andersenpress.co.uk

2 4 6 8 10 9 7 5 3 1

First published in the UK in 2022 by Andersen Press Limited
First published in the United States of America in 2022
by Hachette Book Group, Inc.

British Library Cataloguing in Publication Data available.

ISBN 978 1 83913 324 4

Printed and bound in Great Britain by Clays Ltd, Elcograf S.p.A.

FOR MY MAAME,
BARBARA ELAINE JOHNSON ALEXANDER,
WHO TOLD THE BEST STORIES

MY CHILDREN GLIDED ON THE GREAT RIVER

OVER THE DEPTHS OF DEATH...

THEN, ONE DAY, SILENCE...

—DAVID DIOP

ASANTE

BONWIRE

KUMASI

OFFIN RIVER

UPPER KWANTA

LOWER KWANTA

PRA RIVER

CAPE COAST CASTLE

CAPE COAST

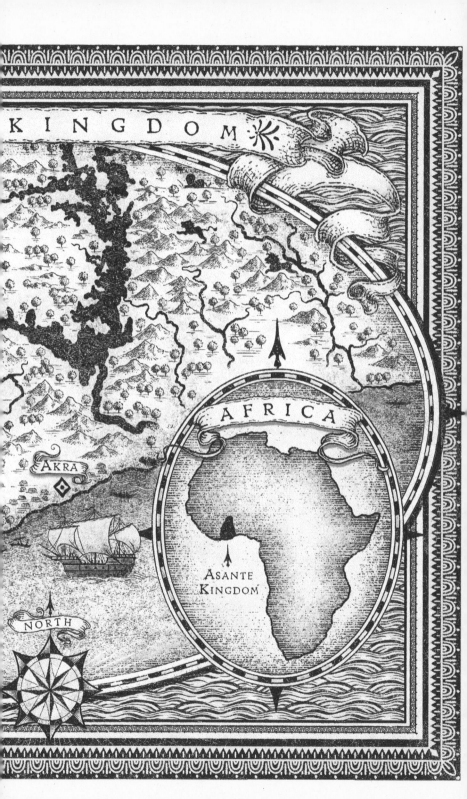

A NOTE FROM THE AUTHOR

This is historical fiction. It is a novel inspired by history, based on the real lives of the Asante (*A·shan·ti*) people, who are native to a region of West Africa now known as Ghana. It was a hard story to write, but it was one that needed to be told. I wrote it for the me nobody knows. For the you who is still becoming. For the possibility that is in *us*. The great poet, philosopher, and abolitionist Ralph Waldo Emerson said, *Be an opener of doors*. I've tried to be that here. Now you must walk through. With your eyes unshut. With your heart unlocked. And your mind as free as the mighty sea...*Akwaaba!*

ASANTE
KINGDOM

SEPTEMBER 1860

CHAPTER ONE

THE STORY OF OFFIN

There was even a time…many seasons ago…when our people were the sole supplier of the purest and most valuable gold in the world…The river was bedded with enough gold to make a century of royal stools for the Asante kings…A thousand shiny bracelets for their wives…Then came the foreigners…Invaders disguised as friends…pretending to be students of our way…with only one lesson to learn…how to steal our fortunes…But we fought them off…protected our rich land, our river…the Offin River…It flows to the east, into the mighty Pra, which travels over one hundred and fifty miles down to the Coast, where it drains into a vast blue unknown that we call the Big Sea... On the rolling sides of Offin are deep forests and farmlands and villages and a boy of the same name... You see, on the morning of your birth, eleven years ago, your maame squatted at the edge of the water, and... Offin carried her fifth child on its shoulders at first breath... It is true, I was there, that you stopped crying as you floated off like a ship inching toward the horizon... The river Offin grabbed you with an invisible cord wrapped around each moment of your day... held you like a mother cradles a baby... pulled you like the moon does the earth... Ever since, you and the water have been bound... river and son, wave and flutter... That is how you got your name, my grandson...

THE STORYTELLER

There was even a time
is how my papa's father,
Nana Mosi, the village storyteller,
begins most of his
fireside tales

always starting
in the middle
of a thought
like we were to know
what *even* came before

always speaking
in slow,
deliberate spurts
about the past
like it lives
in him,
like it still matters

always repeating some things
and pausing at other times,
with a toothy smile

that raises one eyebrow,
right before
the thing he knows
we cannot wait
to hear.

Though he is nearly eighty now
and seldom speaks,
when he does,
I hang on to all his words,
the lulls in between,
and I remember
the stories
like a pigeon remembers
its way home.

IN THE DREAM

I sprint across
the clearing,
past a leopard
teaching her cubs
how to count to ten.

After I grade them,
I dart between the maze
of forest trees
and discover a pot
of boiling plantains
by the river.

Picture me running
over rocks and grass
swept up in the cool breeze
rushing to the water
diving off the back
of a—

SCHOOLED

Offin, how old was
beloved Queen Victoria
when she became heir
to the throne? Mr. Goodluck Phillip, our teacher,
    asks,
startling me
out of my dream.

My cousin,
who thinks he is better
than me at everything,
giggles, then shoots
his hand up fast,
but Mr. Phillip is talking
to me, staring
at me, daring
me
to answer incorrectly.
I will like Kofi Offin
to answer the question, please, he says.

Dunwõtwe, I proudly answer,
standing among

my classmates, smiling
like I just bit into
the sweetest mango.

I do not see
the lightning
almost slice
the skin
from my palm,
but I do feel the scorch
of the rod
across my hand
and in my bones.
I even taste its sting
in my mouth.

Queen's English, please, Mr. Phillip says,
as calm as rain, like
he did not just attack me
with his jagged cane.

Eighteen, I say quickly.
That is correct. The Queen was eighteen, he adds,
        looking at the whole class,
when her uncle died

of pneumonia,
making her the rightful heir.

I am not teaching you
to count in English for nothing.
Sorry, Mr. Goodluck Phillip, I say,
looking down at the purplish welt
burning my sable skin,
and trying not to cry
in front of everyone,
especially Ama,
and my cousin,
who now looks like
he is happily eating
my mango.

OUR TEACHER

Kwaku Ansah
was sent
many, many seasons ago
to Akra
to attend
The Queen's Missionary School
at Osu for the Propagation
of Better Education
and Improved Language,
and when he returned
he had "improved" his name to
Goodluck Kwaku Phillip,
and insisted
to the Council of Elders
that we needed
to be propagated
as well.

ON A MISSION

OUR TEACHER

Mr. Phillip seldom smiles,
is lanky and tall,
wears wire-rimmed glasses
and big-collared shirts
with strange bows
around his neck,
frowns when he speaks our Twi,
insists that we call him
by his new names,
does not like
riddles or bean stew
or most things
we are used to
in our village,
and swears
that he has been anointed
to rescue us
from our old selves
and help us discover
our true ones.

MY OLDER BROTHER

Kwasi once told me
that Mr. Phillip informed
his class that
English is regularly spoken
in Akra and on the Coast,
and if we want to become better,
learned men and women,
we must learn
to speak
this mother tongue,
and when a boy responded,

> *I do not know about your mother, sir,*
> *but my maame speaks Twi*

the entire class erupted
in laughter,
including the boy,
until Mr. Phillip's cane
slashed his buttocks
so hard
he was unable to sit
for three days

and it left
a long, thin gruesome bruise
that swelled
across his buttocks,
making it look
like he was smiling
from behind.

LIGHT SENTENCE

The punishment
for my crime,
for answering
in my own Twi
instead of talking
in the stale, foreign language
that Mr. Goodluck Phillip
makes us speak
in school,
is to stay
after school
so that he can teach me
to read
from *The Dramatic Works*
of William Shakespeare,
which I enjoy—though
I cannot let him know—but
which I can barely focus on
because I want to be in the river
and my forearm is throbbing
and I cannot stop thinking
about the end of the day
when Ama came up to me

and whispered,
But you knew the correct answer, Kofi,
so do not feel so bad,
and her breath smelled
like honey
and pine
and possibility.

AMA

I have known her
since we were
giggling babies
swathed in cloth
on our maames' backs
while they sold yams
and cassava
at the market.

We played together,
learned together,
swam together,
even dreamed together
about our futures
until hers was nearly ruined
when her parents died,
leaving her homeless
and alone.

So, now I mainly get
to see her in school,
since she spends
the rest of her time

cleaning
and being the house girl
for her uncle's family
in exchange for food
and a roof.

AFTER SCHOOL

When we finish reading together,
Mr. Phillip makes me repeat
different English words,
praises my efforts, then says
that if I want to be
a young man of intellect
I should pay attention
to where my tongue lies
when I roll my *R*s,
and even though
I hate the taste
of his alien words
on my tongue
I just nod
and say,
Thank you for
the instruction, sir.

WAITING FOR ME

outside
is Ebo,
my best mate,
leading a band
of youngsters
in search
of the few
gold specks
still swimming
in the streets
and ditches
after last night's
heavy rainfall.

TAKEN

Ama walks
toward me,
carrying a large water pot
on her head,
a bundle of timber
in her arms,
and her baby cousin
draped across
her back.

It will not hurt long if you use this, she says,
placing the timber
on the ground and
taking my arm
in her hand.

She rubs my bruise
with a large, fuzzy, green leaf
and a flash of warmth
rushes through me
like a wave.

I do not feel

my eyes closing, but
I can feel every hair
on my body
jump at the sun.

Is that better, Kofi?
Yes. It. Is.

*Now, do not swallow this or you will cough until you
    die*, she says,
handing me the leaf. I cannot tell whether she is
    serious or not.
. . .

*It is a joke. It is just a clove leaf, mainly used to
    make the pain of a bad tooth go away. You will
    be fine.*
It has the smell of something in my maame's stew . . .
    Thank you, Ama.

Are you and Ebo going to swim now?
If the river is you, I will swim . . . is what I wish I
    could say. Instead, I answer, No swimming today.
    It is too dark.

WHERE I GO

each day
after school
is both hideout
and oasis.
It is where I am student
and king.
A place that holds me
and my destiny safely
in its deep-blue arms.

The river

    where I splash

        and splish

            and kick

into twilight

until the stars emerge
or Kwasi
comes growling
like a hippo.

KOFI, OUT OF THE WATER, NOW!
IT IS ALMOST DARK!

Sometimes
I pretend to not hear
him telling me
what to do
just because
he is older
and bigger,
but when it comes
to swimming,
I have to listen,
because all the elders
in my family
and mostly all
the old people
in our village
say that the river
is cursed
at nighttime.

CONVERSATION WITH EBO

CHALE! Ebo hollers, handing me a palm full of red
    berries.
Just in time—I can use a sweet snack.

Also, I collected these, he says, showing me a bag of
    kola nuts.
What, you are preparing our dinner now, chale? I
    say, laughing.

Oh, these are not for you to eat.
What are they for, then?

*For you to present to Ama's uncle when you ask to
    marry her,* he adds, laughing.
You are a nut, yourself.

Your obsession is so obvious, Kofi.
I am not obsessed.

You are. And you are afraid to tell her.
I am not.

Then do it, big man, tell her how you feel, he says,
    peeling away the kola's white skin.
How I feel? You sound like my sisters.

Ei! Your sisters are smart. And beautiful, he says,
    looking way too excited.
My sisters are married and their husbands will skin
    you for thinking those thoughts.

*Only two are married. Esi is free, no? She is dark
    and comely. You think she will come to me?* he
    says with a smirk.
Ebo, you are a fool.

So, tell me, what was Goodluck's penalty? he says,
    chewing away at the kola seeds. *Did he make
    you hold a stack of books over your head and say
    your numbers in English?*
No, we just read.

Torture.
In truth, it does not bother me. I actually enjoy it.

A witch has cast a spell on you, chale.
To be, or not to be, I say in my best Mr. Phillip
    imitation.

Ei! Speak Twi! We are not in class.
Ebo, how much gold did you find?

I promise you, barely a crumb.
At this rate, you will be an old man with a cane and
    no hair before you collect even a Benda of gold, I
    say, laughing, then turning to leave.

Then I will die rich and happy with my one Benda,
    he says, laughing too. *Ei! What about the river?*
I cannot swim today. I must get home.

I will walk with you, then. In case your cousin and
    his herd are waiting.
And what will you do if they are?

I will run for assistance. HELP! HELP! I will
    scream, he says, laughing.
You are a true friend.

Seriously, do you think I have a chance with your
    sister?
Daabi, I tell him, shaking my head. Not in a
    hundred seasons.

TROUBLE

When I arrive
at our compound
Kwasi and Nana Mosi
are seated
on opposite sides
of an ivory game board,
playing Oware.

So focused
on winning, which
no one has ever done
against Nana Mosi,
Kwasi does not
even look up
when he tells me
that everyone
knows of my wrongdoing
because my cousin
came around earlier
singing
like a guinea fowl.

AFTER LOSING

three straight times to our
grandfather, Kwasi finds me
counting in English.

CONVERSATION WITH KWASI

Mr. Goodluck Phillip is still miseducating his
    students, ei?
He says he is on a mission to widen the sea of our
    intellect and understanding.

He is on a mission to capsize our culture, I promise
    you.
Nana Mosi beat you again?

Our grandfather has been playing Oware for nearly
    one hundred years. He is unbeatable. This I
    know.
He just needs better competition probably.

You are the one with jokes, he says, laughing. *It*
    appears that I am not the only one with an
    adversary.
Can you teach me to punch like you?

Fighting is not the answer.
That is easy to say for someone who fights as well as
    you do, Kwasi.

You have a sharp mind, little brother. Try using that. Outsmart him.

My thoughts are no match for his fast legs, or his powerful fists.

But there are things you have that are powerful. Use these.

What kind of things do you speak of?

Am I to come up with every answer to your problems? Figure it out.

. . .

You must face this, head high.

But what if I—

Ei! The bird who dares to fall is the bird who learns to fly!

What does that even mean?

It means that Maame is looking for you, and she is not pleased, he says, laughing, then tapping me on the head and walking away. *You will be fine. With our cousin, I mean. Not with Maame.* He laughs again.

. . .

PUNISHMENT

I am banished
to bed
for the night
without drink
without dinner
by my maame,
who is only silent now
because she plans to wait
to unleash her wrath
on me
when my father,
who is away
mining,
our business,
returns.

GOLD DIGGER

During the rainy season
Papa leaves
before the sun breaks
and works
two full days
panning
for gold
along the banks
of streams,
leading dives
into the rapid river,
and scooping up
shiny pebbles
and golden nuggets
with a shovel
that he invented.

WHEN I WAS SMALLER

before my schooling began,
he would take me
with him,
sit me on the riverbank
while the women
filled their large trays
with sand
and gravel,
and washed it
over and over
till all that was left
were shiny specks
of gold to be dried
in shallow calabash bowls
under the sun.

I would sit there,
captivated
by the sparkling dust,
watching him
paddle in boats
carved from tree trunks,
plunging

in and out
of the water,
swimming like a fish
in Offin.

I would sit there,
quietly staring
at the horizon
wondering
what lay beyond.

WHEN MY FATHER RETURNS

after the next sundown
both my parents scold me
in the worst way

with a never-ending lecture
on discipline
and responsibility

telling me,
It is when you climb
a good tree that we push you.

What does that even mean? I think,
and what does it have to do
with Mr. Goodluck Phillip caning me

for speaking Twi
instead of English?
So I just nod in agreement.

Papa shakes his head
and leaves.
My maame now smiles,

then hands me
an orange-and-red kente cloth.
I got it at market.

*You will wear it
on the opening day
of the festival.*

Thank you, Maame!
*Ei! YOU WILL NOT SPEAK THAT FOREIGN
    LANGUAGE IN MY HOME.*

Medase! I quickly say, showing my gratitude in our
    Twi, and thinking I cannot win for losing.
*Come, I boiled fresh yam for you and Kwasi. You will
    eat, yes?*
Yes, I answer, taking a bite,

looking grateful,
not wanting to hurt
her feelings.

WE PLANTED YAMS

in the dry season
and now the stems
are yellow,
which means
three things:
the yams are finally ripe,
we will celebrate
the harvest of the yams
at Bayere,
the annual Kings Festival,
and for the rest
of the rainy season
I will be eating yams
until I choke.

THE KINGS FESTIVAL

is eight days
of no school

of plays
about Anansi the trickster spider

of kente costumes
and plenty-plenty of tasty food

of loud drumming
and competitions

of lots of bowing
to the Kings

and the Paramount Chiefs
and all the other chiefs

of honoring
the departed

of prayers
for protection
and prosperity

of lengthy speeches
about our future
and the past

of remembering
the big war.

CHAPTER TWO

THE STORY OF
THE BIG WAR

There was even a time... nearly two hundred seasons ago... when the villages of Upper and Lower Kwanta lived as one family... The land was vast... its crops, plenty... The water was wide enough for each of our people to wash, to drink, to swim... together... We shared the river... and the endless pieces of gold resting in the basin... until, one day, a week's worth of mining went missing... Now, this is where the story gets complicated... It was suspected that two men from Lower Kwanta had stolen the gold and traded it with foreigners on the Coast... So, the King of

Upper, Nana Manu Bambara II, went to see Nana Nii Boateng, the King of Lower, who was drinking and entertaining foreign guests... King Boateng, embarrassed in front of the foreigners, his "wonderfuls," did not take kindly to being accused of harboring the criminals... An argument ensued... insults were thrown... and battle lines were drawn... It was a horrible war... many men were killed... homes were ruined... life was interrupted... until our King got very clever and blocked access to our land (as if land could be owned), to its rich soil, to the harvest, and, thus, to their food supply... which led to their hunger... a truce... and a treaty.

THE BAMBARA TREATY

In order to avert the horrors of war
this treaty is made
and entered into
between Upper Kwanta,
its dependencies, and heirs,
and Lower Kwanta,
its dependencies, and heirs.

1st   There shall be perpetual peace
between both parties,
and neither party shall
have any claim
upon the other.

2nd   Upper Kwanta shall have authority
over the river and its gold deposits,
to be stored in an undisclosed location,
but the King of Upper shall guarantee
a fair, annual distribution
of twenty-five Benda of gold
to Lower.

3rd   The King of Upper agrees not to block
the harvest, and shall permit
Lower farmers to cultivate,

for the purpose of instituting
normal production of crops.

4th   The Kings agree
that the villages shall convene,
befriend, compete, and feast
together at a Festival
to occur annually
in honor
of this peace treaty.

5th   And finally, in the event any subject
of Upper or Lower does violate
this treaty by an act of disrespect
or any crime of magnitude,
a joint Council of Elders
reserves the right of punishment,
to be dealt with
according to the laws
of our people.

DISPUTE

They are the wretched of the earth.
They do not stand a chance
in the festival contests.
We will once again destroy
the lowest scum, my cousin hollers,
tossing a ball around
during our lunch break
in the courtyard.

They are us. They dream like we do. They wake like
we do. They eat like we do. They are us. No more, no
less, Ama interjects. *You should really pay attention*
in class.

A crowd forms around them
as rain begins to dribble
from the grim sky.

They do not eat as well as we do,
and they never will, silly girl, he continues,
getting a few laughs. *And I do listen*
to the lessons.
Upper won the war.

Lower lost.
They are not us . . . THEY. ARE. YOU!
Our servants.

SHE IS RIGHT, THEY ARE US, I shout, before I
  realize what I have done. Ama smiles at me. My
  cousin scowls at me.
Do not butt in, little cousin, unless you want some of
  this wahala, he says, balling his fists.

I do not want any of *this trouble,* I think, as a
  classmate, thankfully, distracts him.
I have heard they are building a big wall. A fortress,
  in case there is another war, says the mate.

Do not be stupid. They are not that smart. But if
they do come for us, my father has the big gun,
remember, says my cousin, aiming his finger at me
and Ama. *Plus, we have all the gold, and he who*
owns the gold eats first, and eats best. That is the
only lesson that matters.

Without hesitation, Ama shakes her head
like she feels sorry for him,
then fires back
with a might

that could lift a log.
*The mind of a fool is like a broken pot. It holds
nothing.*

Everyone laughs
at her mocking
of him, loudly,
including me,
which pricks him so much
he comes over
and punches me
in the belly
so hard, my whole body collapses,
and I spew
my lunch.

Who is the fool now?

AMA JUMPS

in my cousin's face
and calls him
the meanest thing
she can think of—*ABOA!*—which
really is not that bad,
because my cousin
probably believes
he actually is
an animal,
king of his own jungle,
always roaring
and wreaking havoc
on me.

He lifts her
off the ground
as she screams,
trying to break free, then
he
kisses
her.

He. Kisses. Ama.

You know you like that, little house girl, he says,
dropping her.

MY COUSIN

does not walk around,
he marches, thinks
he is a soldier,
is stronger
and taller than me
by two coconuts,
which I have seen him
nearly split open
with his hard head,
then offer to
whichever girl
he is fond of
at the time.

He outran me
last spring
from the village
to the river's edge,
and is so big and tough
he is allowed
to chop timber
with the big men.

But none of that matters
right now, because
Ama has been disrespected,
her honor plunged
into the damp red clay,
and I think I understand
what Shakespeare meant
when he said,
Love never did run smooth.
Forget peace.
This means war.

THE BATTLE

I run into him
headfirst
with the force
of a million thunderstorms
and knock him down.

I do not need Kwasi
to train me, I think.
I am an able hawk
hunting my prey.

The thud
of his back slapping
the wet ground
delights me
tightens my will
brings a loud silence
and sends the heads
of our mates
jerking back
in disbelief.

This had been my strategy
in the few moments
that my heart grabbed
all common sense
and held it hostage:
catch him off guard,
attack like a wildcat,
straight and quick.
Injure him
just enough
so he cannot retaliate,
do any more damage
to her
to me.
What had not been my plan
was him lying there
dead,
then coughing
his way back to life,
and laughing
and jumping up,
wiping the mud
from his back,
wagging his finger
at me,
then chanting the war song

that everyone knew
and loved
and shouted back
to him:

Ose Yie
      OSE YIE
Ose Yie
      OSE YIE.

And when the singing stopped,
the silence erupted.

A TALE OF TWO BOYS

He was born
one week before me,
has won every contest
between us
and even though
we both know
our mothers
will kill us
for *behaving like savages*,
my cousin wants blood:

Mine.

EULOGY

With arms flailing
like wings on a vulture,
he dances
around me
like the warriors
we will both soon become.

And then he pounces,
his fist slamming
into my jaw,
his arms somehow managing
to lock my head
before it hits
the ground.

Me. On my knees,
in his clutch,
each breath shorter
than the one before.

I cannot breathe.

Him: *Before you die, remember this...*

I REMEMBER

the wind whistling
and a cloud of black birds
circling above.

I remember
him turning my neck
to face Ama.

I remember
him whispering,
She will be mine.

I remember
I want to tell Ebo later
that dying feels worse
than I ever imagined.

And then I remember
his arm tightening
around my neck
and right before
my eyes close,
I remember

the sun melting
into nothing,
the pouring rain,
and the voice
of Mr. Phillip
scattering everyone
and saving me
from certain death.

CONSEQUENCE

You are not savages, Mr. Phillip chides,
making the three of us
stay after lessons
and listen
while he teaches us
to read *Henry VI* aloud,
each of us playing
a part:
My cousin, King Henry,
Me, Richard,
and Ama, Margaret.

Goodluck enjoys this entirely too much.

CONVERSATION WITH MR. GOODLUCK PHILLIP

We are each sent home
at different times—first Ama,
then my cousin, then,
since I am a repeat offender,
me.

But before I can leave
he makes me sweep
the entire classroom,
stack all the journals,
and arrange our chairs
in a perfect circle.

The elders will gather here tonight before the start of
*   the festival*, he offers.

. . .

I keep working, hoping
that upon my release
there will be enough light remaining
for me to meet Ebo
at the river.

Kofi, you are clear-sighted
with a good head. There are places
it can take you, if you do not squander
your smarts. Unlike your barbarian cousin,
who has the ambition of a toad.
He is not that bad, just a bit ratty at times, sir, I say,
      not knowing why I am defending him.

He will be an old man one day, in this village,
living a life of regret at what he was unable
to do. Do you desire the same?
. . .

I want to say the most important thing
is to continue reading the texts I offer
and deepen your study, then one day
you too may attend a missionary school.
Perhaps you may even be lucky enough to leave this
      place, okay.
But Kwanta is our home, the Asante, our people...
      sir.

You must think bigger than the Asante, Kofi Offin.
We are the Gold Coast.
Our waters can take you to other places,
other wonderful worlds

far away from here
with learned men
and masters of opportunity.
One day, you will see.

...

But first you must culture yourself.
Until the elders allow me
to officially teach the Queen's language
you will need to learn on your own,
for that is the only way you will sharpen it.
Do you understand, Kofi Offin?
Yes, sir.

You will take the book home, yes?
Yes, please.

...
Thank you, sir.

That is all.
May I go now, sir?

Good day, Kofi Offin.
Goodbye, sir.

JUST IN TIME

I race down
to the river
where I find
a throng of mates
flopping
in the waters
splashing
each other
and Ebo trying
to ride
a strip of timber
upstream.

You really should make one of these, chale, he yells
   at me.
I am fine just swimming, I answer, trying to hide my
   jealousy of his board, before diving in.

THE BIG ROCK

There is a place
far out,
away from
people
watching,
where the water
is crystal clear,
its stream, smooth
and steady.

This is where I go
to swim
and think.

FINGERS FIRST

I leap into Offin
from a tree
head following
feet bouncing
barely breaking
the surface
arms flapping
with the flow
the whole of me
gliding toward
the middle
of the river.

When I get to the big rock
I flip around
and swim back.
On my third trek
I float in the current
stare at the copper sky
think about Ama's scent
and her smile,
then float away,
letting the current carry me

letting the warmth
of the fading sun
bathe me
as I watch it completely disappear
like a dream.

DUSK

I hear my brother
hollering
at us
from the riverbank like
an angry hyena
for me to get out
of the water
NOW!

CONVERSATION WITH KWASI

Maame does not want you near the river at sundown.
It is just turning dark. Why is she always so
    worried? I am fine.

You are only fine until you are not. It is not safe for
    a boy.
I am almost a grown man. I should not be treated
    like a child.

The river does not care how grown you are.
You know I am a swimmer. You have seen me.

I have. You are fast . . . for a schoolboy, he says,
    grabbing me by the head.
This schoolboy can beat you—that I know, I say,
    pushing him off me.

Still, you must be careful.
I can take care of myself.

I am just the messenger, little brother. There are
    things about the water you do not know.
Like what?

The beasts.
The beasts?

Yes, they have long necks and small heads and they
    live under the river, only coming up at night
    because their skin burns beneath the sun.
Brother, you are kidding?

They are massive. If you listen, you can sometimes
    hear them in the forest, he says, stopping
    in his tracks and cupping his hand to his
    ears...
What is it, Kwasi?

...feeding off human flesh...especially troubled
    boys who do not listen to their mums, he says,
    laughing loudly. *How can you be so smart, yet so*
    gullible?
I did not believe any of that.

Oh yes you did. You should have seen your bulging
    eyes.
What is for dinner?

Yams, of course.
I am so sick of yams.

Also, fish, okro stew, and kenkey.
Kenkey is so awfully plain. The most unpleasant.

That is because you refuse to dip it in the pepper. It is heavenly.
For you, maybe. That pepper sauce is too hot for me.

Ei! What do you mean, TOO hot? Are you not Asante?
I will just eat fish.

It is your loss. But anyway, we are celebrating me this evening.
What do you mean?

I have some news.
Tell me.

It seems that your big brother has been chosen to represent Upper Kwanta.
Represent, what do you mean?

In the wrestling contest.
Ei!

CHAPTER THREE

THE STORY OF THE WRESTLERS

On day six of the Kings Festival, the annual wrestling contest between the villages takes center stage... Upper Kwanta's best men face Lower Kwanta's best men, and our best women, theirs... The fighters are tall and solid as oak... the elders drink rum and make wagers on who will be victorious... the women bring cheer through song and dance... and families come together in unity... It is a time of merrymaking... a time of joy... a time of feasting... and a time of fierce battles... in the clearing a few kilometers from the village... lasting from midday to dusk... At the end, champions are adorned with golden bracelets and cowrie necklaces and carried through the village like kings and queens on palanquins...a parade of villagers follow behind, pumping their fists, roaring war cries, singing praises to the two victors...and mocking the losers mercilessly...These contests are the one occasion where Lower can one-up Upper... So, they come prepared and ready to not only win, but to dominate, and when the drums sound, their pride is on full display...

A MIDSUMMER NIGHT

In my dream
the rain spills
from the night sky
like an overturned bucket.

It crashes
against my head
and the water.

Then it stops
and I am a spider
racing my cousin

in the river
and a crocodile
is chasing

both of us
until the crocodile
becomes a leopard

and the river
becomes a forest
and we are running

and my cousin trips
and falls
like a ship
sinking
and I climb a tree
and all I can do

is sit on my eight legs
still, watching
the beast
tear my cousin's limbs off
as he looks up
at me, eyes drowned
in fear
crying for my help
as my maame's voice
echoes
inside my dream
telling me
to help him
NOW!

THINGS MY MAAME SAYS

KOFI OFFIN MENSAH! GET. UP. NOW!
You will sleep until the goats come home if I let you.
You will go with Kwasi to fetch wood.
Ei, boy! Do not make me use the cane on you.
Your sister has made bean stew and pounded yam.
Ahhh, he lives at the sound of food.
Be sure to thank your sister.
And after you eat, you best clean your teeth until
*   they gleam.*
We must not be late for Bayere. It is your brother's
*   big day.*
Ei! I SAY GET UP! No more dreaming. Is THIS
*   world not enough?*

NANA MOSI SAYS

Dreams are today's answers for
tomorrow's questions.

Why do old people speak
in riddles? I wonder.

Maybe we only dream
because of too much
beans and yam.

AFTER WE FETCH THE WOOD

for Maame
I race to the river
and swim furiously
shoulders lifted
every movement clean
every muscle
in my arms and legs
dancing
in rhythm
to the way
of the water.

I race in the river
farther
than I have ever swum before
with so much speed
and force, it is like
I am chasing something
or being chased
when an idea hits me
and I realize that maybe
Nana Mosi was right

because inside
my dream
might have been the answer
to my biggest problem.

THE BIG IDEA

My cousin is
a better wrestler,
a faster runner,
and stronger
than me and Ebo
put together.

One time,
after the fireside tale,
Nana Mosi got a pain
in his back,
so I ran to get Kwasi
and my father,
but when I got back,
my cousin had lifted him up
and carried him
to the home
of the local healer.

But there is one surefire way
that I can outshine him
once and for all,

and I cannot wait
to tell Kwasi
and Ebo about it
later today
at the festival.

WHILE EVERYONE WAITS

for my sister Esi
to finish braiding
and wrapping
my great-grandmother's hair
for the festival,
I sit in the courtyard,
watching closely
as Nana Mosi
handily defeats opponent
after opponent
in Oware.

OWARE

The game starts
with six holes called huts

on one player's side of the board
and six on the other.

Opponents begin
with four stones

in each hut,
for a total of twenty-four per side,

and take turns
picking up stones

in any hut
on their side

then moving
from hole to hole

dropping
one stone at a time.

Land a stone
in an empty hut

and your turn is up.
Land a stone

in a hut
with three others

and you get to keep all four.
The goal is to capture

the greatest number
of stones as possible.

When that happens
the game is over.

THE SILENT WAY

Nana Mosi and I
follow behind
our entire clan
as we make our way
to the festival clearing
for the wrestling contests.

Mostly silent
as we walk, he chews
on a twig,
plucks herbs from stems,
smelling some
and bagging most.

When he does speak,
he starts talking
in the middle
like our conversation
has been going on
all along.

CONVERSATION WITH MY GRANDFATHER

Do not be captured.
What do you say, Nana Mosi?

You have been watching Oware for a long time.
What have you learned?
You count with your eyes, not your hands. You
always go first. And your first move is always the
third hut.

Why do you think that is?
I have not figured that out yet.

Keep watching.
Can you just tell me?

By trying often, the monkey learns to jump from the
tree.
Again with the riddles, I think. I will keep learning,
Nana Mosi, I say.

Take this chewing stick, he says, handing me one
similar to his own twig.

I have already cleaned my teeth, Nana.

Not good enough, he says, shaking his head. *A
    toothless man has nothing wise to say.*
I do not understand.

*Take care of your teeth, Kofi, while you still have
    them. Do you understand that?*
Yes, sir.

. . .

. . .

So, what is this squabble, this family feud I hear of?
What do you mean?

*Ei! Do not play sheep with your grandfather. I am
    too old, and too tired.*
. . .

What is happening between you and your cousin?
. . .

I have asked you a question.
He taunts me. You do not see it, but he does.

These are the games that boys play.
He is not playing, Nana. When he punches, it is
    real.

I remember that my own brother used to hang me in
    the air by my legs.
What did you do?

I stared at the ground, held my arms toward it so I
    did not crack open my head when he dropped me,
he says with a smile.
This is not funny, Nana. It is torture.

You must not let him get to you.
That is easy for you to say. I am the one being
    bullied by that barbarian.

Ei! Watch your tongue. A family tie is like the river.
    It can bend, but it cannot break.
Mr. Goodluck Phillip says he is uncivilized and will
    live a life of regret. I believe it.

Goodluck, with his ridiculous name, knows nothing.
    He is lucky to have a job.
He is my teacher, so he must know something.

*This is the same instructor who insists on teaching
   you to talk like a stranger.*
He says one day we will need to know the Queen's
   English.

*We will not abandon the Asante legacy of dignified
   language.*
He says we are the Gold Coast now, and that a
   wonderful world awaits me beyond our waters.

*You listen to me, Grandson. Do not be swayed by his
   civilized brow. We are and will always be Asante.
   These wonderfuls he speaks of are invaders. They
   will trample on the very red soil he walks on.*
What do you mean, *these wonderfuls*? Invade what?

Ask your papa.
I have asked both him and Maame about many
   things to which they say I am too young to ask
   so many questions. Why keep me in the dark?
   Speaking of the dark, why must I only swim in
   the river during the day?

*Your mother is right. You ask far too many questions
   for a boy so young in age.*

Soon, I will have my ceremony to become a man.
   Then you all will not be able to deprive me of
   knowledge.

*This is true. Do you think you are ready to cross
   over?*
Of course I am ready, Nana Mosi. I get stronger each
   day.

*I am not speaking of your body, but of your mind.
   There is much responsibility with knowing,
   Grandson.*
...

*Soon, you will hunt and marry, and before long,
   after many, many seasons have passed, you will
   be a wise sage walking at a snail's pace through
   life, telling tales and sniffing herbs like your
   nana,* he says, laughing.
You think I can be a storyteller like you?

If you are a dreamer, young Kofi.
That I am, Nana.

SIGNALS

I tell Nana
about last night's dream
of the crocodile
and the leopard
and my cousin
in need
and how real
it all seemed
especially his eyes
so full with terror
and pleading
for my help.

Nana Mosi stares
at the tops
of the trees
for what seems like forever, then
he says,

Kofi, we dream
to heal
our memory
or to face

the unimaginable truth.
Dreams are hints
from the beyond,
but they can also be warnings.

Then we go back
to walking
in silence.

IN THE SHADE

under a coconut tree,
chewing on the twig
Nana Mosi gave me,
I see Kwasi, standing
as grand as a king,
assured, like he is ready
for anything,
chattering and charming
the group of wrestlers
from our village
who laugh and live
on his every word.
When he catches my eye,
he gives me a thumbs-up,
and I know one day
I hope to be as bold
and brave
and captivating
as my brother.

WHEN EBO ARRIVES

he eyes me, stops dead
in his tracks,
and waves me over,
because ever since
he was hit
by a falling coconut,
his fear of trees
is as huge
as the knot was
on his head.

So I get up
and go to him,
eager to tell him
of my big plan.

UNDER OUR BREATH

we snicker
at the talkative old man
from Upper
who has no teeth,
at the woman from Lower
whose colorful headgear
is bigger
than a boat,
at the crowd of jolly people
waving their burning sticks
of cedar incense
in the air.

Even Mr. Goodluck Phillip is in
a festive mood.
He greets us
as he walks by
and after we finish jeering
and laughing
at his bizarre red outfit
and the thick, braided ribbon
lying on his chest
like a fancy necklace,

we make our way
to the front
of the crowd
where dozens
of other boys and girls
impatiently await
the start
of the first matches.

So, what do you think of my plan, Ebo?
Chale, I must say, it is the best idea you have ever
had. You are a big fish, your cousin is a minnow.
He does not stand a chance, he says, stuffing his
mouth with red berries.

CELEBRATION

The festivities kick off
with the band
of drummers playing
as men and women
from each village
take turns
honoring the harvest
and entertaining the Kings.

The circle of spectators
cheer wildly
when one masked dancer
from Upper
performs a spider-like routine
on his toes
that is so dazzling
no one dares follow.

Then the drumming stops.

FACE-OFF

The announcer calls
everyone to attention.
AGOO! he screams.
AME! we scream back.

Then we watch
as the women fighters
with short, cropped hair
painted red
jump, kick, choke,
and try to squeeze victory
out of each other
in the dozen moments
that each match lasts.

REVERSAL

FACE-OFF

The last women's match ends
when a brawler from Upper
with enormous legs
longer than me
gets tackled
but somehow
rolls on top of her opponent,
wrapping her legs
around the girl,
then flipping her over
so ferociously
that when her head
slams against the ground
the poor girl
is out cold.

The reward
for Long Legs
is song
and dance
and loud clapping,
plus gold bangles
and a basket

of kola and groundnuts,
which she hands out
to all of us
as she towers
through the crowd
on her victory march.

WHILE WE WAIT

for the sound
of the horn
that signals
the first men's match,
Ebo tells a joke
about a flying lion
but right before he gets
to the funniest part
someone taps me
on the shoulder.

AMA

If you were a mango
I would peel you

Keep you for myself
then reveal you

If you disappeared
I would find you

Treat you like gold
and then mine you

If you were a secret
I would carry you

between my two lips
and then marry you,

is what I want to say
to the girl

who makes my stomach wobble
and my heart beat

like a drum
but what actually comes

out of my salty mouth is
Would you like some nuts?

CONVERSATION WITH AMA

Ete sen.
Hi, I say back, practicing my English, even if a bit
nervously.

*You do not have to be afraid to speak Twi with me. I
do not have a cane.*
...

That is a joke, Kofi.
I know.

How is your arm?
Better. It does not burn in the water anymore.

Well, that is a good thing.
...

Well, I must go now.
WAIT, DO NOT LEAVE, Ebo shouts.

What is it?
Kofi has something to say to you, he says, nudging
me.

It is . . . nice . . . to see you.
Kofi, it is nice to see you. Thank you for the nuts.

. . .

. . .

That girl really smashed the one from Lower, my
    cousin squawks, coming from out of nowhere
    with his herd of rowdy mates.
I hope she is okay, Ama answers.

Our village won. That is all that matters.
What matters is that she be okay, Ama says, turning
    away from him, toward me. *Well, goodbye, Kofi.*

Bye, Ama, I answer, wishing my cousin was the one
    leaving.
That is not his name, says my cousin.

Of course it is his name, Ama replies, turning back
    to face him.
I am Kofi first.

You can both be Kofi, she says.

Ei! But not THE one and only Kofi Katari, doer of all things great. That is me. Am I right? he says, turning to his mates.

KOFI! KOFI! KOFI! they chant, pointing at him, like the followers they are.
OFFIN! OFFIN! OFFIN, they whisper, pointing at me and laughing.

Tell him, Ebo says.
Tell me what? my cousin replies, now standing in my face, his hot, rank breath piercing everything pleasant inside me.

It is nothing, I say, letting fear own me again.
I did not think so, Little Kofi, he says as Ama shakes her head and leaves.

NAMES

My youngest sister was born
on a Sunday, so she is Esi.
My brother is Sunday too,
so he is Kwasi.
Ama means Saturday-born.
My uncle is Kobbie
for Tuesday,
but everyone addresses him
as *The Mayor*
since that is his job.

You see, we are each given
first names
for the day
we came
into this world,
and extra ones
for the spirit
we brought along.

My cousin and I
were both born
on a Friday,

so we are both Kofi, but
since he is slightly older
two inches taller
and a promising tyrant
who thinks he is the sun
and everything revolves
around him because
his father is the Mayor,
and his maame, the Queen Mother,
he often gets his way,
which includes calling me *Offin*
or *Little Kofi*
and tormenting
everyone else
into doing the same.

THE DUEL

Just as he starts
to walk away,
Ebo hollers,

KOFI KATARI! WE CHALLENGE YOU!

My cousin turns around,
tilts his head to the side.

What is it you say, Ebo?
To the big rock and back. He challenges you to a
    swim contest, Ebo says, nodding toward me.

Is this true? You think you can outswim Kofi Katari,
    envy of little boys, leader of others, future King of
    the Asante?
KOFI! KOFI! KOFI! his mates chant again.

Kofi darts through the water like an arrow, Ebo
    continues, making it worse.

My cousin walks back
toward me

wagging his finger
in that way I hate
with a smile
that I fear.

Little Kofi Offin wants to race me in the river, he
  says, knocking the nuts out of my hand, and
  crushing them with his big, ashen feet, *then,*
  water boy, we will race. In seven days . . . We. Will.
  Race.

CONVERSATION WITH EBO

WHY DID YOU DO THAT?
Because you would not.

I was waiting for the right time, Ebo.
Time lost is lost forever.

I am furious.
That is good. We will use it for inspiration.

I will use it to pop you on the head.
*You must start standing up for yourself, speaking
    your truth.*

My truth? What are you, a sage now?
*I am only saying that you must find your confidence
    and wear it proudly, chale.*

Do not call me friend.
This is what you wanted, no?

Yes, but—
*Then we will train every day. You will own the river.
    He will go down!*

. . .
Say something.

But there is nothing to say
because the wrestling is beginning.
The men are being presented
for battle
and once again
Ebo has made a bed
that I will have to sleep in.
UGH!

THE PROCESSION

The fighters stand
in a small circle,
twelve young men—six from Upper,
six from Lower—looking outward
at the crowd,
rubbing palm oil
over their arms
and shaven heads,
across their chests.

Women and men
from both villages cheer
on opposite sides of the circle,
eat nuts,
guzzle beer
from large gourds,
and shout foul insults
like they loathe
each other.

The drums sound
and the first opponents,
chosen by the Kings

of each village,
begin circling each other
slowly, then faster
like hawks hunting
for prey.

LEGEND

Bonsu, the big fighter
from Lower Kwanta,
who won
the last two Bayere wrestling contests
by flattening
each of his opponents
on the first approach,
knocking others unconscious,
and leaving the unlucky rest
maimed
for life,
is the contest favorite
and a callous giant
with hands even bigger
than his rival's head.

While he swaggers around
pumping his fists
in the air,
hyping up the spectators,
his smaller opponent,
in an effort to capitalize

on this seeming distraction,
runs toward Bonsu
with all the speed
he can summon
and rams his head
into Bonsu's stomach,
then tries to grab his leg,
lift him up,
and throw him
to the ground.
But none of this works.
He bounces off Bonsu
like a flea.

The giant towers over him,
kicks him repeatedly
in the ribs,
all the while taunting him.

Then when he is tired
of mocking,
Bonsu bends down,
takes hold
of the tiny wrestler's neck,
hoists him up,

locks his head
until the boy's eyes roll back,
then ruthlessly slams
him to the ground
to seal the win.

UNMATCHED

Prince Yaw Boateng,
a show-off fighter,
who happens to be
the nephew
of the King of Lower Kwanta,
greets his opponent,
then immediately gallops
like a wild animal,
jumping
and shouting
a war song.

By the time he is ready
to fight
his opponent is so dizzy
from trying to keep up
that he cannot stop
Prince Yaw Boateng
from grabbing him
from behind
and squeezing him
so hard
that it takes all his breath away
and he faints.

TAKEDOWN

My brother
wrestles like he plays Oware
all strategy and planning
and outsmarting
his opponents
who grow so tired
of chasing him
that they practically give up
opening the door
for a slew
of lethal strikes
and graceful takedowns
that seal
his first three victories.

CONGRATULATIONS

My father is proud,
my mother will not stop hugging,
and Upper Kwanta cheers
my brother
for making it
to the final match.

Even though I am happy
for him,
I am also worried
because it is inevitable
that he will have to face
the heartless giant.

*It was a gallant effort, but he should forfeit now if he
    is to face Bonsu*, Ebo says.
Ei! What do you say? The giant still must defeat
    Yaw, I answer back, mostly trying to convince
    myself.

BONSU VS. YAW

The King's nephew
lands a few surprise shots
and even grabs
the giant's wrist
and twists his fingers
to escape a hold,
but he is unable
to take him down.

When Bonsu grows tired
of putting on a show,
of playing around,
he simply clasps his arms around
the Prince's waist
brings him to the ground
and does not let go.

Now normally, he would try to squeeze
the life out of his opponent,
but when the Prince surrenders
by tapping the ground
with his open palm
Bonsu lets him go

because Yaw is the only son
of the sister
of the King of Lower
and heir to the Golden Stool
and if he suffered any serious harm
in the contest
heads would roll.
Literally.

KWASI SAYS

he is not scared
because the giant
has two feet
like we do,
sleeps and wakes
like we do,
wraps a cloth
around his waist
each day
the same as us,
and eats just like
everyone else.

Yes, but the difference is, his cloth is mammoth and
he eats PEOPLE like they are stalks of corn, I
say. Be careful, brother.

DOOM

Foaming at the mouth
with a wide-eyed grin,
and beating his chest
like a maniac,
the giant hops wildly
around Kwasi,
until he lands awkwardly
on his left foot
and something cracks
like a twisted tree branch,
only he is the tree
and the branch is
his ankle.

Bonsu's jaw drops
almost to the ground
and right before he falls
he lets out
a grueling, earsplitting scream
that sends babies
into their maames' arms
and the birds
way up
into the graying clouds.

INJURED

Unable to walk
Lower must replace Bonsu
or forfeit the match.

KWASI VS. PRINCE YAW

The drummer bangs
a slow, steady
> *Konn-konn*
>> *Tinn-tinn*
> *Konn-konn*
>> *Tinn-tinn*

as the wrestlers pound fists
and kneel in a bent stance
with one knee
on the ground.

Nana Mosi says
that it was once customary
for the winner of the men's contest
to take the winner of the women's
for his wife,
so that the children
would exceed
their talent.
Those old ways
have been abandoned
for a simpler prize:
the winning fighter

receives ten Benda of gold,
and his King,
tenfold that.

At the blast
of the horn,
Yaw leaps,
clapping both feet
in the air,
electrifying the crowd
and surprising
even my brother
with his spryness.

Kwasi rises
from his crouching position,
tries and fails
to grab hold
of Yaw.

The sun is fading,
the air is thick
with the smell
of boiled nuts
and burning cedar,
and the promise

of pain
and triumph,
and when Yaw throws
his head
into Kwasi's head,
and knocks him
to the ground,
the people of Lower roar
with approval.

HUMILITY

Once, when Kwasi and I
were playing Oware,
Maame brought me
a bowl of boiled plantains
to snack on.

Each time Kwasi captured my stones
in the game
he would jump up
and dance in celebration, so
the first time I got his,
wanting to be like my big brother,
I did the same.
I took even more stones
and I celebrated even more,
as he watched me,
shaking his head.

Eventually, my luck ran out
and he beat me
again, but at least
I had my boiled plantains

that Maame cooked
for me especially.

As he walked away
the victor, I looked
into the bowl
and it was empty.

Ei, KWASI! Why do you steal my plantains? They
    were not yours.
Little brother, do not let your cockiness blind you, he
    said, laughing, with a mouthful of my snack. *Let*
    that be a lesson to you.

Yaw boasts,
does backflips
to show off
his coming victory,
but in the middle
of his rejoicing,
Kwasi turns his head
to me
with a confidence
written across his face
that I could only wish for,
and winks.

LAST MAN STANDING

My now-smiling brother
slowly gets up,
begins chanting the war song too,
which startles Yaw
and everyone else.

The drummer's pace quickens
as they square up.
Kum-PUM PUM! Kum-PUM PUM!
Yaw attacks again
and again
but this time
Kwasi dodges him
left and right
until it is obvious
that the Prince is growing
annoyed.
Kum-PUM PUM! Kum-PUM PUM!
Kum-PUM PUM! Kum-PUM PUM!
With both fists clenched
in the air, Kwasi
lunges at Yaw.

They lock arms
around each other's necks,
trading shots to the ribs.

Kum-PUM PUM!
Kum-PUM PUM!

Then, in an electrifying series
of moves, Kwasi somehow manages
to throw an elbow
right above Yaw's heart
that does not quite take him out
but bowls him over enough
for Kwasi to get underneath
and backflip Yaw
over his shoulder
into the earth.

KUM-BOOM!

And then the music stops.

COLLAPSE

We all watch
in slow motion
as Yaw
lies there silent,
eyes bulging,
body limp
like he is disappearing
·from himself.

His uncle, the King, looks stunned.
His maame wails,
blanketing the soundless clearing
like her heart is breaking,
and Kwasi, silent
like the rest of us,
stands over him,
uncertain of what to do
next.

CHAPTER FOUR

THE STORY OF
THE DRUM

*Just as the body has the heart to pump life throughout
it...our village...our nation...has always had the
drum to feed our soul...It is the heartbeat of our people...The dundun drum...The dondo drum...The
konn-konn sound comes by striking the drumhead...
with a hand or a stick...Since even the beginning
of time...we have used these instruments...to make
music and entertain...to honor the Creator...and our
ancestors...to celebrate marriages and victories...to
mark births...and deaths...and rebirths—like the
initiation you will soon face...In times of war...we*

have used the drum to call to arms...to power our soldiers' emotions...to ready them for battle...Our drums talk...and it is also true that they sometimes send important news...messages...Learn these...as you would the songs your maame teaches you...They are played to inform you...to protect us...

THE DAY FOLLOWING

the competition
it is typical
for the men to roast a pig
in the ground.

There would be
barrels of groundnuts,
mountains
of sugar bread,
slathers of meat,
and unlimited mango.

The two Kings
their chiefs
and their councils would
drink themselves blind,
then laugh and haggle
over small things
in daylong gatherings,
while most of the kids
play water games
and the mothers
knit and prepare food
for the Grand Feast.

But this day boasts
no pig roasting
or mango
or swimming
or playing
or haggling,
because the heir
to the throne,
the Lower King's nephew,
has been killed
in the annual Kings Festival
wrestling contest
at the hands
of an Upper,
and so, the joint Council
of Elders
will convene
at the town center
to determine
my brother's fate.

REMORSE

Kwasi sits
in a corner,
muddled,
still visibly shaken
not saying a word
not eating a thing
not knowing
what will happen
to him.

Kwasi, are you okay?
...

THERE IS NO COMFORT

for my maame,
whose moans and cries
are loud and long,

nor for my sisters,
who sit at her feet
and spoon her tea.

Even though Papa
keeps telling her,
I promise it will be okay. The elders will know it was
    an accident,
Maame is convinced that Kwasi
will be put in the stockade,
or made a servant
to the King of Lower
to pay off the debt
of human life.

Our compound is being guarded
by a handful of armed men
for fear of retribution,
which my maame thinks
is inevitable.

ADJOURNED

Near the end of the day
we hear the drum
signaling the verdict.

Commotion swells
outside our gates.

We rush to find
a crowd forming
as Lower's King,
his chiefs and elders
march out of our village
in a fury
shaking their heads
spitting on our ground
and hauling accusations
at the elders
from Upper's council.

THE DECISION

In accordance with
the Bambara Treaty
of 1787, and
the laws of
Upper Kwanta
and Lower Kwanta,
it has been decided
by the joint Council of Elders
in a vote of five to four
that the killing of Yaw Boateng
was neither an act of disrespect
nor a crime of magnitude,
and that it was a matter
of unfortunate accident,
and therefore no punishment
shall be enforced.
While Kwasi shall not be held negligent
of the death,
in order to keep the peace,
Upper will be fined
twenty-five Benda of gold,
five sheep,

and two goats
to be awarded to the King of Lower,
as apology.
So it is written, so it shall be.

THE ACCUSATIONS

You call this justice? It is wicked barbarity!
You Upper fools are blind and ignorant.
That was no accident!
A slap on his wrist for murder!
To hell with your bloody apology!
You cannot exchange sheep for a life.
You disrespect him by not calling him Prince.
TWENTY-FIVE BENDA OF GOLD FOR
A LIFE? Ei!
Do not think we will sit idly and accept
your ruthless deeds! Be sure of that!
The heart never forgets what the eyes
have seen!
The God we know does not reward evil.
Long live Lower. Down with Upper!
You have made your bed. I hope
you are ready to sleep in it.
HEADS WILL ROLL!

HOPE

Papa insists that the King
and his men
are just angry
and their fury will subside
and they will get over it
soon enough
and the people will be fine—ours
and theirs.

HENRY VI, PART 3

To me, it seems
like the King of Lower
is as serious
as Margaret when
she stabbed Richard, the Duke of York,
and declared,
Off with his head.

I just hope that
chaos and revenge
do not cause suffering
because of these
ruthless deeds.

GATHERING

BACK TO SCHOOL

The thick smell
of tomato and onion
and smoked fish
is rich
in the air.

The feast
in our courtyard
to honor
my brother's victory
and acquittal
is loud and delicious, but
after Kwasi complains
of a stomachache,
Nana Mosi
prepares Kwasi a clove
to chew on,
and chamomile tea
that puts him to sleep
for the whole night,
and he misses
his own party.

BACK TO SCHOOL

The gong is rung
and we rush
to line up
outside the schoolroom
in rows of ten
for inspection.

Agoo! Mr. Phillip mutters, like the word itself
    disgusts him.
AME! we answer.

Ama's friend Sanua
is sent home
for wearing beads
around her ankle.
Another mate, for not bowing
his head during
morning prayer,
is booted as well.

Ebo and I quickly swallow
the last of our hidden red berries,
before we too are caught
breaking a rule.

We all greet
our teacher
in unison:
Good morning, Mr. Goodluck Phillip. How are you?
then sing a morning song,
which is never the one
we can dance to,
the one our maames taught us
to love:

> *chay chay koo-lay*
> *chay chay koo-lay*

but is always the boring one
about a fair lady,
a man who smokes a pipe,
a bridge called London
that keeps falling down,

or

the one
about the little star
that twinkles
yet no one seems to know
what it is,

which is baffling to me
because the song tells you
what it is:

IT. IS. A. STAR!

AFTER MORNING ASSEMBLY

we march inside
to begin another foreign history lesson
on the Queen's coronation
in 1838
at some place
called Westminster Abbey
and all I can wonder is
why we do not spend
as much time
learning the history
of our own kingdom.

CHITCHAT

Mr. Phillip
is called outside
by an elder,
granting us
a moment
of freedom,
leaving us to talk
quietly
among ourselves.

LITTLE KOFI

has challenged me
to a swimming contest,
my cousin announces
to the whole class.

Kofi Offin is fast. He is like a fish in the water, one
    boy says.
Ei! If he is a fish, I am the whale, my cousin
    answers, laughing.

You better watch out. The last boy who challenged
    a Mensah boy did not fare well, says one of his
    chums.
If only Little Kofi were as strong and bold as his big
    brother, but you are not, right? my cousin scoffs,
    wagging that finger at me again.

When will this race be? another student asks, joining
    the eyes all staring at me.
In five days' time. Come one, come all to witness
    my mate destroy and crush Kofi Katari, Ebo
    blurts out.

I am beginning
to question
my judgment
in friendships.

AFTER LESSONS

Ebo and I trail
Ama and her mates
to the river
to fetch water.

*Do not worry about the race. I have seen your cousin
      swim, and he just kind of rolls around in the water.*
It is easy to judge standing on the shore, Ebo.

And he kicks like a frog.
I hope you are right.

Do not hope, chale. Know. Believe!
. . .

A taami tree, look, Kofi, he says excitedly.
More red berries . . . great.

You will not sneer when I shoot up like a cypress.
I do not believe that a berry will help us grow taller.

It is a magic berry.
Yes, but—

No buts, *chale. Believe, and see it happen.*
. . .

We are far enough behind
so that the girls
do not know
of our presence,
but near enough
to hear their giggles
and watch the rhythm
in Ama's cheerful stride.
Her bounce bewitches me.

Bewitch? What are you saying, chale?
I was speaking to myself.

Well, speak lower, lest they hear us, he whispers
as we duck
behind a tree.

HIDDEN

The tree we climb
stands in perfect view
of the stream
where the girls
dip their feet
and play
before filling
their pots
with water
and carrying them
atop their heads,
each with one hand
tightly holding it
in place.

Ama removes
her hand from the rim
to scratch her arm
or slap a mosquito
or something,
does not put it back
and still moves
across the ground

like a dancer,
never spilling
even a drop,
her head still
as the water
it holds.

When they get beneath
our tree, she stops,
and the other girls do too.

You can come down now, she says,
placing her pot on the ground,
and looking up
straight at me.

CONVERSATION

Ei! How did you know we were up here? Ebo says.
*We have known you were following us since we left
    school.*

I told you to be quieter, he says, shaking his head at
    me.
We were just, uh, keeping an eye out, you know.

So, you are our protectors, she says, smiling.
. . .

. . .
*Well, now that this is settled, can we go for a swim?
    We must practice.*

So, it is a fact you will race Kofi, ei? she asks me,
    ignoring Ebo.
Yes, I will.

And he will lose . . . if we are not prepared, Ebo
    hollers, heading down to the river.
What is your reason for this challenge, Kofi?

I, uh, I, I just want to show him that he is not the
best at everything.
The lion's power lies in our fear of him.

I am not afraid of him. He is a bully. And he thinks
he is bigger and better. I will show him!
...

...
How is your brother?

I worry he may never forgive himself, that he will go
mad with guilt, you know.
Everyone knows it was an accident.

I do not know if that matters so much to Kwasi.
I hear him sobbing in his sleep, and the few
moments he is awake, he just stares, silently,
with a dazed look.
...

...
My family prays with yours.

Thank you.
I should get home before the water is needed.

How do you keep it balanced?
*Once you carry your own water you will know the
    value of every drop.*

. . .

. . .

I will see you at school.
I believe Ebo.

What do you mean?
*You will win. Your cousin does not stand a chance,
    Kofi Offin,* she says, smiling, walking away.

LOOK WHAT I CAUGHT

Knee-deep
in the stream,
Ebo tosses
a long-bodied fish
that is still breathing,
even after it lands
on the bank
at my feet.

IT WALKS, he hollers
as we watch it
nearly stand up,
flapping
back and forth.

I pick it up,
toss it back
way over his head,
let the river
swallow it,
watch it flex
and whirl
away.

Then I do the same.

THE FLOW

YOU WILL NEVER BEAT HIM
MOVING AS SLOW
AS A TURTLE, Ebo screams,
like he is my teacher.

You are not my boss, I answer,
taking a break
before launching
into my third stretch.
WATCH AND LEARN, CHALE! I scream.

For hours,
I fly through the water
like a black eagle,
tightly gripping the current
with each stroke
of my arms,
kicking my legs
in sync,
and thinking
about nothing
but the flow.

THE SUN IS BLUE

with hints of red
when Ebo bets me
that he can stay
underwater
longer than me,

then red
with hints of orange
when I finally emerge
a full hundred count
after he does
and see him
pouting
because he has lost
and now has to eat
a dung beetle.

I heard beetles also make you taller, I say, breathing
     deeply,
and laughing out loud.

TRANSLATION

Even though Ebo knows
far fewer of Mr. Phillip's foreign words
than I do,
his spot-on imitation
is easy enough
to understand,
and it has me
in stitches.

> *I will like Kofi Offin to speak*
> *like a goat. Because I am a goat.*
> *The Queen's English is*
> *very, very good,*
> *not BAAAAAAAAd!*

He is on a roll
and I am nearly
on the ground
bowled over
in amusement
by his perfect performance
when we hear a noise,
a whisper

a sigh
a hum.

Chale, shhhh! Do you hear that?
Yes. A talking drum.

Sounds like it is crying.
It is late. We should go.

It grows louder.
It is getting closer.

Do you think it could be—
I think we should run, Kofi.

CHAPTER FIVE

THE STORY OF THE CRYING WATER

There was even a time when the setting of our sun brought shadows from other places... near and far... white shadows who ignored our peace... who arrested our dreams... who clamored for our gold... And they did not stop until they got what they came for... until every speck of gold lined their pockets... The Offin River was cursed... from source to mouth... Many beautiful ones disappeared... they were taken under the black sky and unborn... If you listen closely, you can still hear their wails beneath the water... When

Offin is hungry for attention, there is no crying for mercy, no begging...only demand...And once it has you, you will not return...The water is not your friend, at night...

BREAK

It is my father's day off
so I am allowed
to miss my schooling
and go with him
and Nana Mosi,
first to the market,
then to visit the carvers
who shape timber
into tables
and jewelry
and other precious items.

They surprise me
with a polished mahogany marvel
to mount
the small waves
in our river—my own board
that will dwarf Ebo's.

Next, we head
to the clearing
so I can learn

how to shoot
arrows.

Not to make war, Nana Mosi says. *To be prepared
in case someone else makes it
for you.*

After several rounds
of bad aims
and mis-shoots,
we go to the rapids,
and I lay on the board
stomach down,
let the fast-flowing stream
carry me,
while they sit
on the bank
playing Oware
and talking
until Nana Mosi dozes off.

When I finish
I part with the board
and swim,
but I am unable

to find my rhythm,
the nerves getting the best of me
with Papa's penetrating eyes
fixed on my every move.

CONVERSATION

You are fearful in the water.
I am not afraid, Papa.

I see you struggling. If you grow impatient, you will
*   sink.*
I know.

If you know, then do.
. . .

When will you race your cousin?
. . .

Do you not think I know about this contest?
I, uh—

Kofi, he is your family. Even if you win, you will
*   lose.*
What do you mean?

We are each branches of the same tree. It does not matter
*   that we go in different directions. The roots are one.*

That is what he means, Nana Mosi answers, his
   voice deep and raspy, his eyes still closed.
He thinks he is big stuff because his father is a big
   man. I will show him.

*It is not the crown that sits atop a man that makes
   him big. It is what is inside,* he says, tapping
   the left side of his chest. *Know your heart,
   Grandson.*
. . .

. . .
Papa, what is wrong with Kwasi? He does not even
   speak to me.

He does not speak to anyone.
Why?

A heavy heart seizes the tongue, Kofi.
But it was an accident.

*Still, the thing happened, and a life was lost. Your
   brother must find a way to deal with the guilt of
   that.*
Will he be okay?

Guilt has the footprints of an elephant.
What does that mean?

*He can find his way back, but he will need to be
    stronger than ever.*

    . . .

    . . .

May I ask you a question, Papa?

Another one?
Who are *the wonderfuls*?

    . . .

Did you hear me, Papa?

*It is getting late, we should go. Your maame will be
    worried.*
Papa! Please tell me what it is I ask.

When you are older.
This is what you always say, *When you are older.*
    Before the dry season comes, I will be older, a
    MAN even!

I believe he is saying that the gift he desires for growing
    older is answers, Nana Mosi says, chuckling.
You are mixing my words, Grandpapa. That is not a
    gift, it is a right.

But you are a boy now, my father rejoins.
Stay out of the water at night... Do not walk by
    yourself in the forest... It is like a river of big
    secrets here.

I am in need of a good quiet and a long nap.
    And right now, you two deprive me of both.
    Cannot father and son take a break from such
    quarreling?
...

There are things in our history that you will learn in
    due time. Be patient, my father says to me.
And what if it is too late by then?

He is right, Addo. A history unknown will replay
    itself, Nana Mosi says to his son, my father,
    giving up on his nap. *We must tell the boy what*
    he needs to know, Addo.
You cannot protect me forever, I say to both of them.

My father sighs heavily,
juts his head forward,
stares at me
with a half-smile
that vanishes
when he turns
to Nana Mosi
and nods.

What lies beneath? Nana Mosi asks, gazing at the
    water.
Fish, of course. And gold, I answer. Is that what you
    mean?

A HISTORY

All along the Offin River,
our people traded gold
for sheep and cattle,
and land, he continues.
Soon, we had land
as far as the eye
could see,
and enough meat
to feed us all.

Our neighbors
near the Coast
told us
of new traders
from other lands,
with new things
to barter: sacred texts,
tobacco, alcohol, and
a wonder weapon
that could rapidly spit out
small, round, deadly pellets
of lead.

Our Kings became
spellbound by the wonderful
new traders
and their rum,
and their smoking pipes
and their strange prayers.

Before long,
gold became
the God
of these foreign trespassers
with magical guns,
so they built large, gated castles
along the Coast
to protect
their religion.

But it was not enough.
These wonderfuls wanted more.
They wanted bone.
And blood.
Ours.

What do you mean, they wanted our bone? To eat? I
    do not understand.
Perhaps when you are older you will.

That is enough for one day, Papa says. *Your nana is
    tired. The rest for another time, yes?*
Yes, Papa.

Are you ready to go?
Home?

*No, again to the rock and back. And this time,
    remember to raise your shoulders, and use this,*
he says, pushing on my stomach, *not just your
    arms. Head stable, improve your kick. That is the
    only way you will prevail,* he says.
Okay...Thank you, I say, turning to Nana Mosi, for
    being on my side, for telling me.

*I am only on the side of what is right. And you are
    welcome and deserving. Remember to think of a
    proper gift for your born day that your nana can
    grant you...Now go be an arrow!*
Yes, please, I offer, hugging him, diving into my
    destiny, my mind distracted by sacred texts and
    blood and bones.

RED RED STEW

When we return to
our compound
the tangy smell
of the red palm oil
and ripe plantain
plus the spice
of the bean stew
hits me like a gust
of goodness.

Maame
usually makes
a separate, smaller pot
for me
and only me
since Red Red
is my favorite food,
and Kwasi is known
to take third
and fourth helpings
before I have finished one.

But tonight,
we all fill our bowls
from the same, large pot,
because my weary brother
is still absent.

DURING RECESS

Ebo tells me that
Awo told him
that Jojo told her
that my cousin
has been going
to the river
at daybreak
to practice
long before school
and that his speed
and strength
in the water
are increasing.

SECOND THOUGHTS

Before today,
I was assured
and ready
to be outstanding,

to outsprint,
outstroke,
and outswim
my cousin
with ease

but with this new information
my outlook
on the outcome
has changed
and now
I worry
that I will be outmatched
by him
once again, and

I wonder
if I should pull out
of this contest.

AND THEN I SEE AMA

glance at me
as she leaves the schoolyard

touching her lips
with a finger

giggling
then pointing it

at me
and in this moment of pleasure

I remember
that I am doing this thing

and no amount of fear
is going to stop me.

IN MY DREAM

my red tail beats
like a drum.

It sways
to and fro
in time
with the wave.

I am a snapper
bending its spine
pushing
through the water
like a sidewinding black cobra
in the forest.

Picture me
beneath the blue
both legs
swishing side to side
swimming faster
than I have ever swum
before.

Going
		Going
				Gone.

A torch
in the sky
blazes, and
somewhere
a dawdling fish—eating
lunch, perhaps—is
caught
in a net,
while his friends watch.

THE NEXT DAY

Most times we swim
our heads up
slicing the water
with our feet.

But what if I kicked
side to side, like this,
I explain to Ebo,
twisting my body
from left to right,
coiling
and curving
my arms
like a snake.

You had a dream that you were a snakefish? he says.
I dreamt, I answer, of the way to beat my cousin.

THE FISH KICK

Ebo counts
as I swim
to the big rock
doing my normal stroke,
but on the way back
I break into my new kick
keeping my head
above water,
my arms tight
out front,
and I feel myself
speeding toward
the shore.

This is impossible, he says, looking puzzled.
What?

*Usually, to the big rock and back, the count is
     between 110 and 120.*
What did you count to today?

...
CHALE! What is my count?

Eighty-nine.
Ei!

You are going to smoke him, Kofi.
That is the plan, Ebo. That is the plan.

MANHOOD

Maame comes
into my room
sits at the foot
of my bed
while I practice reading
and reminds me
for the hundredth time
that I am expected
to prepare
a praise song
about growing up
for the crossover
ceremony
that concludes my initiation.

Then she takes my book away
rubs my scalp
and sings to me,
like she used to
at bedtime
when I was a small boy.

Before she leaves,
she asks what I would like special
to eat
at my born day party,
and I tell her
lots of boiled plantains,
but please
No. More. Yams.

And we both laugh.

RIVER RUN

After my chores
I spend the rest
of the afternoon
practicing my fish kick
in a stream
that I thought only Ebo
and I knew about.

Until today.

Hello, Kofi.

CONVERSATION WITH AMA

What are you doing there?
I have come to wash clothes, and then I saw you, she
    says, standing next to a palm, with half a coconut
    in hand.

. . .

Would you like a taste? she asks, handing me
    the coconut. *This one is very, very sweet, like
    paradise.*

Thank you. How do you know about my place?
So, you own the rivers and streams, ei?

. . .

How is your preparation for the battle coming?

It is not a battle. Only a race.
Tell me again, why are you doing this?

I am tired of losing to him.
You are smarter and nicer than he is always.

. . .

You would be faster if you were underwater while you swim.

What do you mean?
I mean that your raised head slows you down.

That does not make sense.
It makes sense to me, Kofi.

But how will I breathe?
When you need to breathe, bring your head up.

. . .

Also, try paddling with your arms, as if they are oars.

How do you know so much about this?
Remember I am older and wiser than you, she says, grinning.

. . .

You do not remember we used to swim together?

I do remember.
I will have to be back soon. Goodbye, Kofi.

I wanted to say thank you.
For what?

My arm is healed.
You are welcome, okay.

. . .

. . .

Tell me something, Ama.
Yes?

How long will you have to be a house girl?
Until I am old enough to take care of myself.

How long will that be?
Another four or five seasons, I think.

What trade will you take up then?
I think I will become a swimmer, or even a wrestler,
    she says, smiling, *and win enough gold to take*
    care of any child who is orphaned.

. . .

Or I will study to become a teacher. What about you?
    What is your big dream?

I think I will be a teacher as well. But I will not be
the kind of teacher who attacks his students with
a rod or cane.
Or the kind who makes them speak an alien tongue.

He is the worst.
Definitely.

Definitely.
Well, I have work to do.

Wait! Will you come in for a swim? Then I will help
you clean your clothes.
What do you know about washing, Kofi?

I wash my body every day, I say, laughing.
Another day, she says, winking with a tender smile
that owns every wet inch of me. *Keep your head
down, Kofi Offin.*

CAPTIVATED

I watch her
walk away,
her crown
of cornrows
reaching for
the sky,
like a tall tree,
and wishing
I were a leaf
or a branch.

But you may walk with me if you like, she says,
    without turning around.

SMITTEN

While she washes clothes,
I scavenge
for shells
and some twine
for a special gift
I will make.

When she asks,
What are they for?
I tell her
for my maame's born day
even though we celebrated that
months ago.

We do not say much more
on the long walk
to our homes
but she does hum
to herself, softly,
and every now and then
my hand speaks to me,
tells me it is lonely,
dares me
to befriend hers.

RESURRECTION

CONVERSATION

For the first time
since the accident,
Kwasi emerges
from his seclusion,
still not saying much,
but practically eating
a mountain of rice
plus every mango
and plantain
he can locate.

After he is stuffed
like a pig,
we kick
a ball around
our moonlit courtyard
just like old times
and then I ask:

A game of Oware next, brother?

CONVERSATION WITH KWASI

. . .
Tell me, are you okay, Kwasi?

I am fine.
It is just that I know you are in pain, and I—

You know nothing of pain, Kofi. Just play.
We are each worried about you.

*You should spend your time worrying about your big
    race. It is tomorrow, ei?*
Yes, I will swim against Kofi.

For the heart of a girl.
No.

It is always over a girl, brother.
. . .

If you win, will you marry her? he says, laughing a
    little.

Why does everyone keep talking of silly things? I
say back, happy to see even a little laugh from
him.

Little brother, you will need to present gifts to her
family. Two goats, a cow, whiskey, and a pair of
sandals for her father.
I am not marrying anyone.

And a piece of cloth and gold bangles for her
maame, he adds, pointing at the huts.
No pointing at the stones, Kwasi. Count with your
eyes only, or game over.

My brother has been watching and learning. Tell me,
has Nana Mosi told you about the two-headed
beasts?
I am not believing in you and your beasts again.

It is known that a lover must go to the land of the
dead and fight three battles against three two-
headed beasts. If he survives, when he comes
back, he must give the tails of the three monsters
to the beloved. That is the sign of true love.
That is a lie.

Is it?
You are just trying to scare me.

. . .

. . .

I think I will be leaving here.
What do you mean?

*It is time for me to start a life, somewhere else. I have
   dreams.*
Dreams? I do not understand.

*There are great kente weavers in Bonwire. Maybe I
   will go there and study with a master.*
But no one leaves Upper Kwanta. We are all born
   here, and we die here.

*There is much more than Kwanta, Kofi. The world
   is a big sea. I want to dive in. Let the wave carry
   me.*

. . .

I need a change. Surely you can understand that.

. . .

...

If you are leaving because of what happened, it is
    not your fault.

...

Kwasi, it was an accident. It could have happened—

JUST PLAY THE GAME.

...

HALF-MOON

Nana Mosi says
when half of the moon
is bright,
and the other half
is shadowed,
we are supposed to let go
of anger
and hurt
and grudge.
We are supposed to forgive
each other.

And ourselves.

CONVERSATION CONTINUED

May I ask you a question, Kwasi?
You are stalling.

Tell me about the initiation. Ebo says it will be
   unpleasant.
*Cutting timber all day under a flaming sun is
   unpleasant. Your initiation will be dreadful.*

. . .

*But do not fret. You will be ready, as we all are ready
   when it is our time.*

What else?
*You will be taken to an unknown place, you will be
   tired, you will be hungry, you will get hurt, you
   will feel like you want to give up, and you will
   not know the men who torture you. That is what
   else. Now, it is your turn. Go!*

Does Maame know you are planning to leave? Papa?
Play!

I am thinking.

Time is running out for you, he says, nodding to the
sand sifting in his glass timepiece.

Why do you have to time me? That is not how I play.

*You want to play with the big men, you play by big
man rules.*

Fine, I say, finally deciding which small stone to
move.

*If you pick that one, I can assure you that the next
move will lead to your capture. Kokoduru!*

I am braver than you think.

*You are playing scared. KokoDURU, little
brother!*

SHUT UP, I am trying to concentrate, Kwasi.

You are trying to delay the inevitable.

It is when you cannot win that you must attack, I say,
making my move.

Nana Mosi's words cannot save you, he replies,
turning up his lip, and studying the board for the
first time with uncertainty.

GAME OVER

*Ei! You are getting good
at Oware,* he says,
as we play to a draw
for the first time,
both of us capturing twenty-four stones.
*But are you good enough
to outrace me to the river?* he says,
galloping away
like a tiger.

THE WOODS

The old trees block
what little light
the moon throws
at us,
but we have run
this beaten path
so often
our feet
have memory,
and we trust
their way.

WHY ARE YOU STOPPING?

I ask Kwasi,
who is staring
up at the branches
of a gum tree,
then back
at its base
like he can suddenly see
in the dark.

What do you see, Kofi?
It is dark, I answer. I see nothing. Why did you stop?

There is a rope trap here.
A rope trap? Do you mean for a rabbit?

This rope is much bigger, and much longer, Kofi.
Why is it there?

*The bigger question is who is it for? And who put it
    there?*
. . .

*If I were not more careful, I would be hanging upside
    down at this very moment.*
Maybe we should go back.

*Ei! Do not be a chicken. Show me how you will win
    tomorrow,* he says, taking off running again,
    toward the river.

ON LAP AFTER LAP

READY. SET. KO!

When we get to the river's edge
I stand in the water,
staring out at Offin
turned all peaceful
beneath the fallen sun.

Kwasi sits on the shore,
leans back
on his elbows, tells me
to make it quick,
because we should not even be here,
because he is hungry
again,
then flips
the sandglass over
and yells,
KO!

ON LAP AFTER LAP

READY, SET, GO!

to the big rock
I fly
even faster
with my head submerged,
but what swims
through my mind
is the time
Mr. Phillip read to us
about Julius Caesar
daring his rival Cassius
to jump into the Tiber River
and race him
and almost drowning
until Cassius saves him,
only to later help
his own brother-in-law, Brutus,
kill him.

All I can think about is
if I do not beat
my cousin,
in my heart
I will have suffered
the same fate
as Caesar.

CALLING

Nana Mosi says
that the rivers are the sacred space
where our ancestors dwell
so that they can assist you
during times of need.

Well, right now
they must think
I need them bad
because as I approach
the bank
I hear the river
bubbling over rocks
and branches,
flowing so loud
it sounds like
they are screaming
at me.

HIDING

CALLING

When I come out
I do not see my brother
lounging riverside
but I do see
his timepiece lying
in the same spot
where he sat,
and even though
I know he is probably hiding
and wants me to find him,
for a moment I grin, thinking
that maybe the beasts
he is always chattering about
have finally come
for him.

SEARCHING

He is not
on the beach
buried beneath sand
waiting to pop up
and scare me
like a ghost...

STILL SEARCHING

He is not spying
on me
behind a palm tree
or perched in it
waiting to jump out
and grab me
like a bandit...

NOWHERE

When I call his name
for the seventh time
there is still no answer
only the sound
of the night winds
roaming the forest
and carrying a silence
now marked by
a familiar fear.

Mine.

I WISH

it was after school

I wish
it was after school and Ebo and I were laughing

I wish
it was after school and Ebo and I were laughing and
trailing Ama

I wish
it was after school and Ebo and I were laughing and
trailing Ama and her friends

I wish
it was after school and Ebo and I were laughing and
trailing Ama and her friends
all the way to the river

I wish
it was after school and Ebo and I were laughing and
trailing Ama and her friends
all the way to the river and when we got there we all
jumped in

I wish
it was after school and Ebo and I were laughing and
trailing Ama and her friends
all the way to the river and when we got there we all
jumped in and Ama and I sat on the riverbank

I wish
it was after school and Ebo and I were laughing and
trailing Ama and her friends
all the way to the river and when we got there we all
jumped in and Ama and I sat on the riverbank
holding hands

I wish
it was after school and Ebo and I were laughing and
trailing Ama and her friends
all the way to the river and when we got there we all
jumped in and Ama and I sat on the riverbank
holding hands and our breath

I wish
it was after school and Ebo and I were laughing and
trailing Ama and her friends
all the way to the river and when we got there we all
jumped in and Ama and I sat on the riverbank
holding hands and our breath until she kis—

ALARM

The loud noise
is a rapid thunder

is the sky crashing
into the river

is a sudden bolt
that strikes

through the air
like a violent storm.

THE FIRST THREE BLASTS

stun me,
stop me in my tracks,
turn my head
to the west
toward its origin.

The next three declare
the deadly bullets
of a gun,
and each of the cries that follow
send me back
through the woods
racing to the east, home,
away from the advancing storm.

HERE IN THE DARK

the trees grab for me
like thieves snatching
and I can see nothing
not the rocks underfoot
not the crushed toad
not the wind on my trail,
but I have to keep moving.

Here in the chilling dark
everything is louder
each trembling leaf
each whistling branch
the hard, hurried thump
inside my chest
even the rush and clump
of my own feet
scares me.
I am alone
and I have to keep moving.

Here in the dark
I am blind to the unknown
running fast,

far away
from the shots
that grow frenzied
and furious.

Here in the dark
I am hoping
and praying
wishing
this is a dream.

But...

THIS

is not a dream.

This. Is. Not. A. Dream.

is not you running
from a leopard
or becoming one

is not a spider
being chased
by a crocodile
or a cousin
or a snake

is not you riding
a blue whale
into the night

is not you perched
on a branch

is not Ebo playing
a joke on you

is not your maame's voice
in the morning

is not the touch of Ama's hand
in yours
or a smile
or a kiss.

This is not you tripping
or sinking
like a ship.

This is you moving.
And then not.

This is you falling
up.

BIG TROUBLE

Upside down
in the new rain
ankles gripped
by a tight rope
drenched body bound
in a web
eyes wide open
sightless
stuck
trembling
dangling above
the earth
like a caught rat
and crying out
for help.

No, this is definitely not a dream, Kofi.
You are very much awake
and this trouble
that has found you
is dreadfully real.

CHAPTER SIX

THE STORY OF THE INITIATION

Our people have always believed that there is a journey the spirit takes...It begins at birth...takes you to manhood...to womanhood...then marriage... and ancestorship...We call these transitions of the mind, body, and soul rites of passage...It is a coming of age into your identity...your belonging...But this is not an easy transition...There is much work to be done...much training before one can cross over to the next stage of life...There was even a time where it was said that if you failed one phase, the elders would determine if you were worthy to begin again...

or not...Kofi, you are soon to cross the bridge from boy to man...Do not listen to the myths—that you will have to cut off your own finger and eat it...or kill a big boar with a leaf...those are childish tales from embattled boys with wild imaginations...No, that is not real...But what is real is that your initiation will be harsh...your hair will be shaved...your body will be marked with ancient symbols...you will be prepared...to protect the women and the children...to uphold what is just...to fight what is wrong...and your will, your commitment to faith...will be tested by the elders in vicious trials...where you suffer... and wish to die...Only then will you become a man of strength and honor...

THUNDER

My hands bound together
by twine,
a tall, dark shadow
holding a machete
yanks me
through the storm
by the same rope
I hung by.

It is too dim and rainy
to recognize the gated village
where they have taken me,
or make out
any of my captors' faces.

But I can hear fine,
and while the sound of rain
thumping the earth
is familiar,
the burst of frightening cries
coming from
the chamber
they lead me into
is not.

GROUNDED

They push me
onto a damp spot
next to five other boys,
each looking
as terrified
as me.

They shackle
one of my legs
to a plank
dug in the center.

One of the boys,
very small,
bobs his head
to and fro,
weakly whimpering
like a mournful wind.

The small-small has been crying since we got here,
    chale, one of the others, a large, burly boy says,
    looking at me. *They told him they will cut his*
    tongue out if they hear him again, he adds.

Where are we? I ask, but he puts his finger up to his
 lips.

Shhhhh! They say no talking, one of the other five
 says to us.

. . .

DETAINED

I try to place
the faces of the men
who marched me here
through forest
and marsh
never uttering
a single word,
and that is when I realize
that none of them
were familiar,
that Kwasi, who is probably
back at home
losing Oware
to Nana Mosi again
or eating all the Red Red,
warned me
that when it is time
for my initiation
I will not know
the initiators,
the men sent
to torture me.

THE DRUNKEN LAUGHTER

of our nightwatch
and the *pap, pap, ka-ka-ka*
Skidiki-pap-pap
of their random gunshots
finally mutes,
which brings
a little relief and hope
that we will be allowed
to rest
before everything starts.

A boy
with swollen eyes
thick with dread
stares through me
like he does not even see
me.

Part of me wants to calm
his panic,
say we will be brave together,
and the other part
wants to turn away

from the numbness
coloring his face.

He is the Zombie. Does not speak or eat, says the
    chubby one. *Look at his eyes, they are empty.*
How long have you each been here?

Some a fortnight, others more or less, he responds. *I
    am Osei, by the way.*
This is a part of our initiation?

What else could it be?
KOMM! hollers one of the drunken men outside our
    keep. *Close your mouths, or I will close them for
    you.*

VISION

There is no opening
for light
in this dank cell,
so when they take us out
each morning
to relieve ourselves
our eyes cannot adapt
and we are nearly sightless
to everything happening
around us.

FOOD COMES

only once a day
spicy soup

with slivers of meat
and just enough yam balls

for us to fight over who
gets the last one.

If this is what it means
to become a man

I want to stay a boy
with heavy-handed teachers

and Shakespeare,
and Oware

and crushes
and yes

more yam.

MEMORIES

If we are to be trained
for adulthood,
why are we caged,
shackled like animals,
I wonder aloud.

We are being tested, Osei whispers, as if reading
my mind, his eyes still closed. *You should be
sleeping to prepare your mind.*

While we wait
for the instruction
that Osei is certain will come,
the sound of the rain
has become
my chum,
the musical backdrop
to better days,
the door
to my memory:

Ebo liked to repeat
Nana Mosi's stories

about Anansi the spider,
because he believed
he was as clever and smart
as the spider.
But are you as greedy too? I would counter,
which always caused great laughter.

I wonder if he, too, is somewhere
awaiting his fate,
preparing for initiation.

Right now,
I would give anything
to chop wood for Maame
or read after school
with Mr. Phillip
or be the ire
of my cousin's eye.

These are all the things
I ponder
until sleep, my ally
of calm,
comes knocking.

IN THIS DREAM

I am a baby again
tied to the broad fin
of a dolphin,
but I am not
in the river.

No, this time
it is a large, mighty water
that drags me
across its gigantic waves
climbing,
then crashing
over and over.

And this time,
I do not know how
to swim,
and even if I could
it would not matter
because
there is no dry land
in sight
to swim to,

and the big fish is hungry
and I am too
and suddenly we stop
and I hear drums talking
as if the mighty water itself is speaking
a nursery of stars
splattering against its skin
faster
and faster
and nearer
and closer
and louder:

The Lion is near the village
The Lion is near the village
Run
Run

The Lion is in the village
The Lion is in—

MY MOUTH!

IN THE BACK

of my mouth
is an unbearable throbbing,
the painful squeezing
of a tooth
that jolts me
awake
in the middle
of the night.

CONVERSATION WITH THE SMALL-SMALL BOY

You have a bad dream.
I look to see where this whisper is coming from.

It is okay, says the small-small, sitting up and
    staring at me. *The men outside have fallen*
    asleep. They cannot hear us.

. . .

Please, Me din de Owuraku but most call me Owu.
I am Kofi Offin, I whisper back, pointing to my jaw.
    It is my tooth that pains me.

I am sorry... Where are you from, Kofi Offin?
Upper Kwanta.

May I ask you something? Why are we here?

. . .

And that is when it hits me
that the strangers
who brought us here
and the boys caged with me

are not from Upper,
and as there is no such thing
as a rite of passage
for small-small boys
the size of Owu
who are very much younger in age
than me,
and since we are shackled
like prisoners,
this cannot be
a challenge,
a game played
as part of some passage
to manhood ceremony.
No, this is something
far worse.

Go to sleep and rest for whatever is next, I urge
    Owu.

Obeying me
as if I were a big brother,
Owu lays his head
on the clay.

You will feel better, I hope, Kofi, he says
as I sit up
holding my jaw,
staring into
the agonizing darkness
of what I now think
is a nightmare.

WAKE UP!

a lanky man waving
a machete screams,
kicking mud onto us.

Along with the other men
he unties
the six of us,
drags us outside
where the sun beats down
and after our eyes adjust,
I see their mohawk plumes,
their sharp, stinging eyes,
and for the first time
the tribal marks
that hide
their cheeks.

CARVED

on the shaven sides
of their heads,
from eyebrow
to below the ear,
are pairs of lines
and patterns
and symbols
that say *Strength*
or *Crocodile*
or *War Horn*
but one of them,
a little man
no taller than me
with a tail of hair
hanging
at the back of his scalp
whose face does not glower
like the others,
wears on his cheek
the shape
of two fish biting
each other's tails.

THE SLOW WALK

The rain slows.
In a tree above,
a perched bird watches,
fluffs it golden feathers,
and sings, *Po Po Po!*

The sound of drumming
grows heavier
the farther they march us
across the mucky grounds
of this foreign place.

It feels good to be hugged
by the sun again,
even if it is just a sliver
peeking
from behind a cloud.

In a courtyard,
people gather,
as an old man
with two small drumsticks
beats out a message
on a giant wooden dondo:

The King is coming
The King is coming
Bring out the prisoner
Justice will be served
Justice will be served
Bring out the prisoner.

REVELATION

We make our way
through a mob of onlookers
sneering at us,
past a woman
crowned by a
gigantic
red-and-yellow head wrap
whom I recognize
from Bayere
from the wrestling contest
from the crowd
of cheering villagers
from Lower Kwanta.

Are we in Lower? I ask myself,
now more confused
and unsettled
than scared.

When the drumbeat stops
the crowd turns to look
at the arrival of two men

hoisting a large canopy,
shading
the returning rainfall
from the King
of Lower Kwanta.

FORTRESS

I am in the village
of our rivals
behind a big wall
my friends and I thought
was just a fable,
and the prisoner
the old man sang of
is a beaten and bloodied man
the marauders throw
at the feet
of the grinning King
like a hurt fish
tossed back into water.

And that prisoner is my brother,
Kwasi.

THE TRIAL

Ei! What will happen when we run out of fingers to
hack? I want to say that it will not be pleasant to
lose your toes also.

. . .

Another chop, says the King, before taking another
   puff of his pipe.
AUGGHHH! NOOOOO! PLEASE!
AUGGHHH!

My brother's screams
scare the songbirds away
pierce my soul
like daggers
drops me
to my knees.

KWASI! Tell them what you know, please, I beg,
   even though I do not know what they ask.
Ei! Even your little brother wants you to confess.

The shock on Kwasi's face
when he sees me

seems to multiply
the pain
of his severed digit.
He just shakes his head
in agony, slowly,
as if the flame
of his injury
just got fanned.

I am sorry, he mouths to me.
What is it you say? the King shouts.

I do . . . not . . . know what you ask, Kwasi moans.
You must. Your father is the head gold digger, is he
      not?

Yes, but—
Then you, as his oldest male heir, would know
      such things, as my oldest heir once had my
      confidences.

. . .

But you, who have taken the life of my heir, you, who
      have evaded consequence, you, whose life is not
      worth to me one Benda of the gold you protect,
      will now stand before me with a chance to make

amends and save your life, yet refuse to tell me
where it is kept. You leave me no choice, then.
STAND HIM UP!

DAABI! HE CANNOT TELL YOU WHAT HE
DOES NOT KNOW, I scream, before I am
quickly gagged.

THE GOLD

After the war
between Upper and Lower,
our King took control
of the gold, storing it
in a secret repository,
whose location
is only known
by three people—the King
of Upper,
his Paramount Chief,
and the head authority
of gold-digging,
who happens to now be
my father.

SENTENCE

In accordance
with the Bambara Treaty, you,
Kwasi Baako Mensah, son of Addo Mensah,
grandson of Nana Mosi Mensah,
who has committed
the heinous crime of murder,
taking the life
of Prince Yaw Boateng,
son of Yaa Boateng,
nephew of King Nana Boateng,
shall be dealt with
according to the laws
of the people
of Lower Kwanta, announces
the King.
Bring out the jury.

ATTACK

The drummer beats again,
summoning
three vicious-looking large men
with arms the size
of thick tree limbs
to the center
of the courtyard.

They form a half-circle
around Kwasi,
who bleeds
from his head
from his legs
from a right hand
that now holds
only two fingers.

I think of Kwasi's fingers
left in the dirt
to be scavenged
by a small, wandering beast.

I think of Maame's worrying
that retribution was certain.

And, for the first time,
I think of the real possibility
of death.

The drum stops
while another man
with a horn
awaits a signal
from the King
to start the match
where my brother
will have to fight
three men.

Between the river
of sadness that
drains from my eyes
I see Kwasi
inside the storm,
dripping
with blood and water
staring at me,
with a grin on his face

and a familiar word
on his lips:

Kokoduru, he mouths.

Then he attacks.

POSSESSED

He rushes one opponent
grabs his left leg
throws him to the ground
twists his foot
as far as it will go
then twists it back
and while he yells
in agony
Kwasi sinks his teeth
into the man's ripe ankle
with the bite-force
of a wild dog
and locks
his bloody jaw.

Then, without hesitation
and in controlled abandon,
he jumps up,
kicks and punches
with such brutal force
and fearlessness that,
even though they outnumber him,
the remaining two fighters

refocus their efforts
on defense,
backing away
from my brother,
to the King's dismay.

Kwasi leaps
and lunges at one,
headfirst into his chest,
then, in rapid succession,
unleashes a flood
of blows
to the other man's chest
until he is down
and out.
He turns,
winks at me,
and I think of
all the tall tales
he has told me
about massive monsters
who battle
and devour human flesh,
and I wonder
if all along
maybe he was the main character

in the stories,
the two-headed beast
living under the surging sea.

The surprise
on the faces
of the crowd
mirrors mine
but not for long.

THE RAIN DOES NOT FALL

on one roof, Nana Mosi says,
which has never made sense to me
until today,
when the King declares,
ENOUGH OF THIS! LET THE GIANT FEAST,
and Bonsu,
no longer hobbling with a bad ankle,
sporting powdered red hair
and wearing iron bracelets
with cutting edges,
enters the courtyard
and gallops sprightly
toward my brother
like a monsoon.

THE FIGHT

Kwasi lunges
at full speed
launching the sole of his foot
right into the black boulder
that is Bonsu's rib
but the giant does not even flinch
just stands there
annoyed
like a mosquito
just buzzed
in his ear.

GET UP

Kwasi is sluggish
after falling,
the back of his head slamming first
into the hard, wet ground.

As the giant stands over him
watching
I feel a kind of silent dread
of what will come next.

Bonsu stomps him
in the gut
then lifts him
off the ground
with one arm
wrapped around
his neck,
carrying
my listless brother
through the courtyard
for all to gaze
and gape upon.

I thrust myself
toward them with all my might
but the thick twine that ties
me to the other boys
traps me in my place,
and its tug knocks me
to the mud.

The one with the fish
on his face
helps me up
as Bonsu lumbers
toward the King,
who seems pleased
that my brother is dangling
like a hooked snapper.

*Tonight, the other world will host
a new visitor,* the King shouts.

Still clenching his neck,
Bonsu lets him down,
lets his feet touch earth.
The drum beats,
Owu closes his eyes,
tells me to do the same,

but I cannot.
I will not abandon Kwasi
so, when the drum stops
and I see the giant
snap my brother's neck
like a twig,
all hope dies
and the darkness
swims
all around me.

IN THIS DREAM

Mr. Phillip, sitting
on the big rock,
reads Shakespeare to me
while I race Ebo
in the water.

Then Ebo is gone,
and I have swum too far,
way past
where the sun dips
beneath the mighty.

I picture Maame and Papa,
and Nana Mosi,
and Ama watching
from the shore, waving me back,
but I am trapped,
and each time I open my mouth
to scream HELP,
a stabbing pain
shoots through it.

I cannot speak.
I cannot move.
I need help.

What is happening to me?
Who can explain to me now, here,
why I am so far away
from everything familiar?

There is nothing more confining,
I hear Mr. Phillip read,
than the prison
we do not know
we are in.

And then I wake up
leaving everything behind
in the dream
except the pain
and the dread
of this cell,
and the memory
of my brother's face.

I THINK PAIN

is contagious,
because the throbbing
in my mouth
has returned
and it is as terrible
as each thought
of Kwasi's lifeless body
dangling.

I can only cry inside
because noise
will bring rage
from the men with guns.

My brother is gone, my brother is gone, I murmur over and
     over, until

the pang of his death, until

the pain in my mouth, until

the weight of my wounded world

is just too much too much to carry

and I have to let it go, let it out.

So, I do.

OUTCRY

My piercing screams wake everyone
but I do not care.

The other boys tremble in unease
and no one tells me to *Shhhhh*.

Guards do not even come rushing in
to threaten us

and if they did,
it would not matter.

Kwasi is dead
and my body can no longer house

the river of tears
swelling inside like an angry morning tide.

I am on the other side of hope,
the place numb to fear.

A place I could have never imagined
that I now live in.

You killed him.
THEY KILLED HIM!

LATER ON

Drink this tea, says the bald one, the one with two
    fish on his cheek, waking me up.
. . .

It will help with the hurt, he adds, touching the side
    of his mouth, then his chest.
. . .

*It is good you have calmed down. More outburst will
    only agitate.*
My brother is dead.

Drink.
. . .

It is your face that will fall off, not mine, he says,
    shrugging, leaving the bowl of tea next to me,
    then picking up his gun.
Why are you helping me? I ask, holding my jaw,
    trying to wish my troubles away.

Two Fish turns back around
and puts his finger to his lips.
Shhh! he whispers, pointing to the tea.

Maybe he wants to poison me, I think,
pondering my kidnapper's motive,
until the tea's familiar scent
passes beneath my nose
and a not-so-distant
calming memory comes
rushing back to me
like a tide
to the shore.

A SOOTHING MEMORY

A bruised arm
A battered pride
A girl's smile
A healing gift
A fuzzy stem
A woody spice
A clove leaf
A sacred touch
A finger soft
A melting heart
A liquid voice
A closed eye
A better day
A soothing memory.

I SWALLOW

the sweet past
to soothe
my bitter present.
The night slips away
taking with it
the throbbing
the grief
the crying,
making room
for a tinge
of relief
and the sounds
of another bound day.

SOUNDS I HEAR

The heavy rattle
of rain dropping

The thundering thud
of trees falling

The blistering crack
of wood breaking

and the hopeless fate
echoing inside

me
and my cellmates.

WHAT I BELIEVE

is that we are prisoners,
some, maybe of war,
others, of lesser disputes,

some here as debts to be repaid,
to become house boys,
servants to the King,
and others, like me,
as consequence
for wronging Lower Kwanta,
who now seek
their revenge.

What I know
is that we are locked
in a dark cell,
our legs fastened
to stakes
in the dirt,
fed a bowl of rice
with only a few mouthfuls
of water
once at dusk.

What I see
is that
because he refuses
to eat
or drink,
two of our captors pry
the Zombie's mouth open
with some two-bladed metal thing
while a third
pours water
down his throat.

ALARMED

The drums signal
the end
of yet another mournful nightfall,
and the beginning of
the same somber sun.

But this morning,
something is noticeably different,
bleaker.

They gag us again,
before they drag us out
in the rainfall
line us up by height
then march us back
to the courtyard
where my brother's life
was snatched away.

THERE WILL BE NO CELEBRATION

no remembering Kwasi
the way we would have

no music
no singing
no dancing
no praying
no eating
no drinking
no laughing
no hugging
no healing
no hoping
no knowing

that Kwasi's soul
will rest
in peace
here
inside the barbarous gates
behind the big wall
of Lower Kwanta.

AS WE SINGLE FILE

out of the courtyard
over the ground
that holds my brother's blood,
near three giggling kids
chasing a grasscutter,
out the towering gates,
past a herd of goats,
around a group of men
cutting timber,
across the river,
away from home
toward some unknown,
I swear
to the ancestors
that when Papa comes for me
when I am free
I will find a way
to avenge
Kwasi's murder
for my maame
for my family

for the whole
of Upper Kwanta.

This, I know.

NIGHTFALL

We only stop
to rest
because our four imprisoners
have speared
a fat, wild grasscutter,
then sat
to stuff
their faces
with its cooked bushmeat,
before freeing our mouths
and dozing off
with their loaded death weapons
still in their clutches
still pointing
at us.

FREEDOM

In the middle
of this nightmare
that is trying to bury us,
that has us becoming
silent and detached,
like our minds
have abandoned us,
I finally know
what I want
as a gift
for my born day.

So, I bow my head
say a prayer
and hope
that the ancestors
and Nana Mosi
are listening.

THE REMEMBERING

Next to the fading fire
our snoring kidnappers started,
we feed
on the leftovers,
pinches of tough meat.

I think of Ebo
and the traps
he likes to set
for grasscutters
and the profits
he splits with me
from their sales.

I wish to be arguing
with my brother
over a bowl
of Maame's boiled plantains.

What I would even give
right now
for Esi's unpleasant cooking

and chiding
from my sisters.

Owu interrupts,
brings me back
to the now,
to the dread,
asks if I have
a story to tell—as if
that is normal, as if
a fireside tale right now
would make it so—and I think of
Nana Mosi.

THERE WAS EVEN A TIME

many seasons ago
when a young girl
named Ama
was about to marry
the richest, smartest boy
in the village.

On the day
of the ceremony
his family presented
their dowry to hers
in the form
of one goat.

The bride's parents
were furious.
THIS IS RUBBISH! screamed the father. *Where are the*
cowrie shells, the cloth, gold?
The mother was so angered,
she fainted,
with one eye suspiciously
remaining open.

This is not just a goat,
the rich man's father proudly stated.
This goat talks.

The mother's other eye opened.
Ei! What do you say?
The rich boy's father repeated his claim.
Our goat, Nimdee, not only speaks,
but he is a sage.
He truly knows everything. Watch.

And with that, he asked Nimdee,
Will it rain today?

Yes, the sky will open rather soon
and the rain will crash against earth,
Nimdee answered, rolling his *R*s
in a way that would make
my schoolteacher, Mr. Phillip, proud.

Those in attendance at the wedding
stood by amazed
that the goat indeed spoke.
Whereas Ama was brimming with joy,
so pleased that she would marry

her lifelong love,
her parents looked upon each other
with eyes of shock
and confused pleasure.
It is true, the bride's father proclaimed.
Your goat can talk. Let the ceremony commence.

Wait one moment, said the mother. *Of course
it is going to rain. A fool can see that there
are shadows in the clouds. Anyway, it is rainy
season. Let us ask it something of meaning
and consequence.*

The rich boy's parents huddled
with each other
and their son,
then the father answered, *Very well, what will you
    like to know?*

FULL MOON

By the time
I get to the part
in the story
where the girl's parents decide
what to ask
the goat
Owu has drifted off
to sleep like
the others
and I am left
in this strange
and unfamiliar place
gazing at the same full moon
that stares down
at my father
and Nana Mosi
who must be searching
for me.

RESCUE

Ye ko! I hear
coming from inside
the big tree
that holds me up.
We go, it whispers again,
this time grabbing my shoulder
like its branches are alive
like its branches are
arms.

Now, says Two Fish, appearing before me.
We must go while they sleep.
Wake the little boy
and the others.
I do not understand, I reply.

Do you want to die like your brother? he asks,
not waiting for me to answer. *Then come. Ye ko!*
But they will—

Before I can finish,
with a heavy hand
he slaps

the doubt
out of my head.
This is your chance! If you want freedom, MOVE!
he grumbles.

So, I do.

FEAR

I quietly begin
waking each boy
while Two Fish removes
the twine
that binds our wrists.

All of us stand up,
careful not to crinkle a leaf
or step on a branch
and make a noise
that gives us away.
All, but one of us.

The small boy,
the one who bobs
his head
to and fro,
is frozen in fear.
He does not move.

Chale, I say, we must run, now.
But they will hear us, and then beat us, or worse, he
    moans.

What can be worse than what has already happened
    to us?
But we do not know what is to come.

And we cannot trust them to wait to see.
I am afraid, Kofi.

So am I. But fear will not stop us today. Now, stand
    up, I say, grabbing his arm and lifting him. We
    must move, now!

Then we creep away
until Two Fish starts sprinting
and we follow,
chasing him
and what looks like
our freedom.

TRAILING

It is only because
his running is clumsy,
his movement stunted,
that I finally notice
Osei appears to be injured.
But there is no sign of pain,
no grimace on his face,
so, while he hobbles along
I keep running.

ESCAPE

After hours of scurrying
through thick bush

over muddy ground
and rocky springs

the Zombie tumbles
holding his ankle

howls loud enough
to scare the owls

to stop our rescuer
in his tracks

and suddenly halt
our escape.

CONVERSATION

You must get up, boy. We have to keep moving.
Can you see his ankle is hurt, sir? It is likely
    twisted, I say.

Twisted or not, says one of the other boys. *We must
    run before they wake.*
*I will not be gunned down because of a weak, mute
    boy*, says another.

Maybe Osei is hurt too, I say, glancing at him. I saw
    you limping back there.
This, he says, walking toward me, both of his feet
    twisted, and pointed inward. *You see, I have
    bumblefoot since I was a baby. But I am stronger
    than a bull. Do not worry about me*, he says,
    laughing.

*Silence. We will have to carry the boy. You two are
    sturdy*, Two Fish calls, pointing to two tall boys
    who share the same face. *Help me lift him.*
*We are brothers. I am Sisi, he is Koshi. Tell me, boss,
    why are you helping us?* one of them asks.

I do not care about your names. I only help you
   because you cannot help yourselves. Ye ko!
Where will we go? I ask.

What were they going to do to us? asks Owu.
You will find out if we do not move faster, he says,
   handing me his weapon. *Hold this, boy.*

Are we far away from them?
Not far enough, chale, says Osei. *I think I hear*
   noises.

QUICK, LIFT HIM, yells Two Fish. Koshi and Sisi
   do as they are told, each holding one of the
   Zombie's arms, while Two Fish grabs his legs
   and takes off running. *MOVE!*

I HEAR SHOUTING

rushing toward us
like a raging tempest
so we pick up our pace

tearing across marsh
while the full moon
bursting with a new hope

leads us
to the familiar sound
of water

to the edge
of a hill
high above

its gentle stream.

TRAPPED

CONVERSATION WITH
CAPTORS

with our backs
to the cliff,
the three vultures
catch us
box us in,
their firesticks raised
and ready
to roar.

Crocodile and Strength point
their weapons at me,
letting me know
if I do not drop Two Fish's gun
they will drop me.

ON YOUR KNEES, yells War Horn,
targeting Two Fish
who refuses
until he is forced down
by a bullet
that pierces
his left leg.

CONVERSATION WITH THE CAPTORS

You think you are a big man with this, War Horn
says, picking up my gun, and pushing me onto
the ground. *Do not be influenced by this traitor
with his ridiculous tail of hair.*
He thinks he is the boss with his patch of fur, adds
Croc, laughing, then slicing off Two Fish's knot
of hair with his machete. Blood trickles from the
slash.

. . .

You have nothing to say, big man?

APOLOGIZE TO US FOR THIS BETRAYAL!
. . .

*Boys, this small man has betrayed his brothers, his
people. You have witnessed his wrongdoing, each
of you, yes?*
It is you . . . who have betrayed your people,
says Two Fish, shaking his head in disapproval,
as we all watch, petrified, but startled by his
boldness.

Ei! He speaks. What do you say?
You have forgotten the way. And you will suffer for that.

I am the one with the gun on your cheek, little man,
    says War Horn. *Tell me who will suffer.*
And, what is this nonsense on his cheek, brother.
    Is it a fish? Croc says to Strength, who does
    not respond, who has never said a word, only
    showing his rotten teeth through a wicked grin.
He has two fish on his face. Maybe we should throw
    him over the cliff, see if he can swim like them,
    War Horn says, which they each find funny.

No one should bite another. What you are doing is
    treason against your souls. You must take these
    boys home.
Do not worry, your soul will go home soon enough,
    little man, Crocodile says, laughing.

To me, to us, Two Fish yells, right before he jumps up,
    Those who stand tall see their own destiny shine.
ENOUGH! War Horn yells back, knocking him down.

Do not test us again, Crocodile says to us.
If you are a fool and try to run again, War Horn
    says, *let us show you what will happen.*

CONSEQUENCE

Like a game,
the three madmen
take turns
ferociously emptying rounds
of death
into the hairless skull
of Two Fish
until he is unrecognizable,
his face disappearing
beneath a river
of red.

WELCOME

It is two harsh daybreaks
and one stormy nightfall
bound wrist to waist
marching in boiling hot
across beaten red earth
then paddling the mighty Pra River
before we finally stop
before we dock
at a long pathway
leading to a hill
that holds
a high-walled
sinister-looking
colossal white castle
at its peak.

The wonderfuls are there, War Horn says to us, with
    a sneer, pointing up to the castle, then shoving
    us out of the cramped boat. *Akwaaba! This is
    your new home.*

AT THE CASTLE ENTRANCE

in front of a
giant, blackened wooden gate
are three severed heads
on spikes
greeting us
like a scene
from Shakespeare
only this tragedy
is real.

I do not even realize
I am crying
until Crocodile yells,
KOMM!

TWO VERY TALL MEN

in white cloths
down to their ankles
with hair braided thick
as the long daggers they clutch
stand guard,
speaking to our captors
in a tongue
that is not my own,
but close enough
to understand.

Ekutu? one of them says, handing
War Horn three oranges,
while the other
turns around to walk
through the gate.

The six of us,
starved and shaking,
our wrists bruised
and painful
from being bound
so tightly,

stand there
waiting
for some unpleasant unknown
watching
as the men snigger
with the guard
and attack
the fruit
like savages, their mouths
dripping with sap
and sick satisfaction.

THE WONDERFULS

War Horn jumps
to attention.

Crocodile and Strength follow,
sprouting up

like rice plants.
They each stand silent

bow their heads
wipe their filthy chins

and simper
like little children

when the other guard returns
marching behind

two grimy-haired,
pale-faced men

in red coats
who inspire awe

in the guards
with their hideous green eyes

and bronze firesticks
that stretch long

as tree branches.
Their accent is strange

and since they talk
with alien words

unfamiliar to our captors,
the tall guards translate.

What is this you bring? You come to us with only
      four, and two cripples? asks one of the red coats.
      No gold, no cacao for the Governor?
Boss, they are good stock for you, I promise. This
      one, says War Horn, pointing at the Zombie,
      has only a twisted ankle. The other one, the
      bumblefoot, is strong as an ox, I promise you.
      We only want a few nice things for them.

It is true, sir. They are young and fit. No illness or
      pox, adds Crocodile.
Tell me, then, what is your price for this cargo? the
      red coat asks.

THE TRANSACTION

Our King, War Horn utters,
requests
twenty-five muskets
twelve pistols
ten stone gunpowder
a basket of knives
one hundred iron bars
a bag of long cloth
a dozen white plumes
some small-small tobacco
a smoking pipe
and five bottles of rum
per head.

Your King is a grabby one, he is, says a red coat. *We*
  will send you away with half. And you keep the
  useless cripple.
But, boss—

The Crown does not negotiate.
You know we have come too far to leave
  empty-handed.

Take it or leave it.
What do you do with them?

. . .

You have taken so many captives, so what do you do
with them? Crocodile repeats.

That is no business of yours, only that we fill your
coffers, barks the other red coat. *Is our trade*
concluded?
Yes please, War Horn says, softly, still bowing his
head like a house boy.

STRENGTH

unties our wrists
while War Horn and Crocodile
collect the bounty.

I turn to see Osei
and wonder
will they let him go now
will they take him back
or worse.

The two tall guards
muscle us
through the gate,
shoving and jabbing
and elbowing and prodding

until the sound of
War Horn's snickering
is replaced
by the roar
and crash
of a mean, mighty water

until we are in the middle
of a courtyard
that holds more pale-faced men
and tree-trunk-size weapons
built into the ground.

until we are forced
to bend our knees
and heads
to their boss.

THE GOVERNOR

of the castle,
their boss,
walks by each of us
slapping
            grabbing
our chins,
forcing our mouths open
with his filthy fingers,
as if he searching
for something hidden
inside us,
beads of foul sweat
from his face
            dribbling
on our heads.

The red coats
push everyone facedown
to the ground
but me and Owu,
seize their arms,
knee their necks,
then one by one

burn a red-hot iron
onto their arms
that sends them
shrieking and twisting
in horror and
a kind of pain
that I can only imagine
mirrors death.

AFTER THE EXAMINATION

the men with no color
douse the five of us
with palm oil,
then give us a cupful
of water
to drink
before they measure us
from toe to head.

Owu and I are dragged
in one direction,
the Zombie and the other two
in another,
and when he steals
a glance at me,
I am unable
to push away
the horror
in his eyes
or the fear pouring
from mine.

DUNGEON

AFTER THE EXAMINA

We are both thrown
into a pitch-black chamber
littered with human waste
that reeks so badly
our stomachs instantly burst,
emptying
on the cobbled stones
that punish
our bloodied knees.

DIZZINESS

When the retching ceases
and my eyes bend
to the darkness,
I scan
the shadows
of our confinement
and find a flood
of blurred faces
dark and desperate
like mine.

I see stunned little boys
I see frightened girls
I see a dark lady
with hair like a rope
holding on to as many of them
as she can.

My mind fades,
tricks me
into thinking
that Ebo and Ama
are here too,

crammed
into the corner
of my imagination.

Then I see nothing.

IN THIS DREAM

a bull is slaughtered.
Its horns become bowls and beads
and bangles
that become chains.

Its blood turns
to red clay.

I use it
to build a home
near the water
for Ama.

We are eating yams
when the soldiers come
with severed cow heads
tied to their belts.

There is music, a black bird
with piercing white eyes
and broken wings
singing in the night.

Maame calls out to me.
The river says my name.
Even the walls speak.
Come, come, they say. *What is done cannot be
undone.*

CONVERSATION WITH THE DARK LADY

Come, come. Give me your hand, says the soft voice
of a woman floating over me.

. . .

Ete sen? she whispers, sounding like a mother
greeting a waking child.
ME KO! I shriek, trying to jump up. I must leave.

We are not going anywhere. Shhh, before they hear you!
Where are we? I ask, faintly remembering a large
white castle and strange-looking white men.

Are they going to eat us? I hear a familiar voice on
my right.
Owu, is that you? Please, are you okay?

*I am scared, Kofi. Will they eat us and make powder
from our bones?*
Do not be afraid, the dark lady says gently. *They will
not eat you. But your noise will bring wahala!*

What kind of trouble? I ask,
as she rubs my shoulder
and places my hand in hers.

GRAVE TROUBLE

The wonderfuls bring misery
and destruction to those
who do not look like them.

Their eyes covet the whole earth
and they see us as shadows
to step on.

They do not care
of our celestial origins,
that we descended
from the Great Good above.

They do not respect
our traditions
our heroic past
the power of women
the wisdom of elders
and spiders
the joy of peace.

They ignore the life-giving palm fruit
for its slippery, sweet profits
and cannot see even a glimmer of gold
for the riches it yields.

They do not care about
honoring the stars or
the magnificent sky
that houses them,
only that they can use it
to guide them toward
plunder.

The mighty river
that births us, to them
is a speedy path
to our destruction.

This place
is not a castle
of anything good.
It is a dungeon
empty of heart
and these alien people
with their wolfish logic
and wicked impulses
will eat at our flesh
until the blood of Asante dries,
and our steady beat is no more.
That is their way.

Since I came here
with child
eight months ago
I have counted
one hundred
and twelve
children
and women
taken from this damp, dark cell
never to return,
and each day
I kneel down
and say a prayer
to Bona, the Great One
that breathes mountains,
that my first child,
my beautiful little boy
who was unborn
days ago
right where you lay,
is near a star
in the sky
reunited
with all
that is good.

INTRODUCTION

She tells Owu and me
that her name

is Afua
that she is from

a fishing village
east of Kumasi

that her grandmother
is so tall she can touch the clouds

that her little sister
was ill

visiting the healer
when the midnight marauders

seized her village
and killed her intended

that she too speaks English
that there are

mostly young girls here
that she is but one of the few older

that we should call her *Auntie*
that there are fifty of us

some speaking
in a different tongue

that she has cooked
for the wonderfuls

in their spacious kitchens
with parquet floors

and views of a big blue sea
that sometimes the pink-faced men

with their dirty hair
and grimy grins

come in the night
and take a girl from this rotting hole

then bring her back
jumbled and sobbing

that she does not know
where the girl has gone

even though I think she does
that each time there has been a loud GONG

and there have been three
since I arrived

everyone is taken
but she does not know where

only that they do not come back ever
and this time I believe her

that she once was
a sister and a daughter

and a lover
who often fished

with her beloved
and once netted

a snapper
so big

it capsized their canoe
and she and her dearest

ended up splashing each other
playing in the water

and forgetting
that they had lost dinner

and for the first time
in a dozen nights

I laugh
a little.

We all do.

DISTRACTION

My tooth has stopped
hurting, or
it has ached so long
that I am used to it, or
I am focused
on my present agony, or
the throbbing
inside my mouth
has been replaced
by the uncertainty
that awaits outside
this cell, or
my brain has been trapped
in a spiderweb
of normal distractions, like
a mosquito buzzing, like
the splinter of the sun
peeking through
the narrow, round hole
at the top of the stone wall, like
the caring of Owu,
who cannot hold down
the soppy food

they hand to us
once a day
on a wooden paddle
through the iron gate
that cages us.

THE HEALING

I give what little water
I am rationed
to Owu.
Drink, I say, this will help, not believing
that it actually will
since he can hardly lift
his head
or open his mouth
to even say
more than a few words.

Kofi, what happened to the goat? he mutters, the
    sweat swelling across his face.
He is fading, making no sense, Afua says, wiping his
    head.

No, I understand. There is a story about a talking
    goat, I say to her.
*Ahh, I see. Stories can heal. Perhaps it may help
    him.*

NIMDEE

We have demonstrated that our goat does indeed
*   talk. Why not approve of their union, and let the*
*   two lovers become one*, says the mother of the boy
to be married.
Ei! You want us to give you our Ama for a goat that
*   knows the weather?*

Nimdee is a wise goat. There are many things he can
*   teach you, show you.*
We will see about that.

What is the question you will ask of him?
I am thinking. Do not rush me, kind sir, says the
    mother of the girl to be married.

. . .

. . .

The day grows long . . .
We have a question, Ama's father says, after
    convoying with his wife.

Tell us.

It is a hard one. Are you sure you do not just want to
    pay us in cowries and timber?

Ask Nimdee, and see your question answered.
Very well, said the mother. *We will like your Nimdee*
    to tell us why there is so much evil in the world.

The son looked at his mother.
The mother looked at her husband.
The husband looked at their goat.
And Nimdee looked at the sky,
then lay down
like he wanted a nap,
with eyes closed
and mouth shut.
No matter how many times
the father begged him
to answer,
he would not speak.

Please, Nimdee, tell them what they ask, said the
    mother.
Oh dear, wise, old Nimdee, answer them, the father
    pleaded.

The son, who had always thought
this whole paying and bargaining
for his bride thing
to be wrong,
but who had loved Ama
since before he could remember,
dropped to his knees,
pleading with Nimdee,
offering to free him
if he would just comply.

Finally, the bride-to-be's family,
appalled by this show of disrespect,
rejected the goat
and the marriage,
and set on their way.

Now, when they were gone,
Nimdee rose up,
drank from a pot of water
brought to satisfy his thirst
and looked
as if nothing had happened,
as if the boy's world
had not just been turned
upside down.

Why? asked the mother.

Why do you forsake us and not speak? asked the
    father.

Why do you make me suffer like this, Nimdee? the
    heartbroken son asked.

Nimdee chuckled
a little,
in a wise sort of way,
then said
to the boy
and his mother
and his father,

What you do not suffer for, you can never truly value.

OWU BURIES

his head soundly
in Afua's lap
and sleeps.

Do you know Oware, Kofi?

She opens her hand,
drops a bunch
of black and white pebbles
onto the ground
next to me,
right into the sliver of light
coming from above.

You are a good storyteller, Kofi.
Medase! My grandfather told me that one. He tells
   me many.

He has trusted you to keep the stories, ei. That is a
   big thing... Tell me about your people.

. . .

MY PEOPLE

My best friend Ebo
has a big mouth
that often gets me into big trouble.
He believes that berries
can make us taller,
but he means well
and is a good person.

Ama's beauty
is matched only
by her wisdom.
She has lived
through much misfortune,
but still she smiles
brighter than a thousand suns
and stands taller
than most boys,
especially my cousin,
who never means well.
But I was to show him up
in the river, before...
before this...

You see, I can swim
like a fish.
The sound of the river
flows through my body,
but what we listen to each day here,
this is the biggest water
I have ever heard.

WHILE OTHERS COMFORT THEMSELVES

with songs
of solace,
Afua and I play the game
as best we can
long into the night
and I tell her
about Nana Mosi
and Maame
and Kwasi
and Hamlet ·
and Mr. Phillip's rolling Rs—which makes
her chuckle again—and when
I have emptied
all my stories
and she has run
out of questions
I ask mine.

QUESTIONS

Nana Mosi told me

of a mighty sea.
Is this it, Auntie?

Will it take us home?
When do you think we will taste yam again?

Why are there no drums, no music here?
Nana Mosi says dreams are answers to questions.

Do you believe in dreams?
Why do they scorch the other boys?

Where did they take them?
Are there men here too?

Why has no one come for us?
Why were the heads on stakes?

How did you last in here so long?
Am I going to die?

ANSWERS

Afua says
that she misses yam too,
then wipes her eye
and reveals
that the severed heads
belonged to men
trying to escape
this nightmare,
that one day
while she was preparing
palmnut stew
in their great kitchen
she saw beneath
the place where
the wonderfuls worship
a dozen young menboys
tall like her brothers
brought here with her
being shoved
into the hole
of a dungeon,
that Owu and I were not
because they keep

the small-small children
with the women,
that she fills her mouth
with stories
to pass each day,
that they remind her
of the times
that were good
and full of wonder
and before I can ask her
to tell me one,
a deafening GONG echoes
and it paralyzes her.

I believe it is time, she says, stilling herself.

CHAPTER SEVEN

THE STORY OF
THE STORY

There was even a time when human beings and spirits were neighbors and one of the things that connected us was story... Before there was even a single written word, there were poems and chants... rhymes and songs... about births and deaths... marriages and battles... Our people would gather around a central fire... and listen to the storyteller... It is in this way that important messages were passed down through the generations... to help people make sense of the sometimes cruel and harsh world... to comfort... to answer the questions the children wondered... why the leopard has spots...why the elephant is afraid of bees...why mosquitoes buzz in people's ears...We told these stories...and many more...to entertain...and enlighten...to preserve our beliefs...and to record our history...for ourselves...by ourselves...This you must remember...There will come a time when you will tell these stories to the ones who come after you...and they will listen like you listen to me...and they will learn...as you must learn now...until the lions tell their side of the story, the tale of the hunt will always celebrate the hunter...Do you understand this, Kofi?

CHAOS

The hurried footsteps
and raucous commotion
from above
get closer
and closer
to us.

Metal clangs
as the iron door
to our cage
unlocks
and opens.

The frenzied, stabbing orders
from one of the thick-braided
tall guards
in white cloths
shouting at us
to line up.

The women scurry
to their feet.

Auntie whispers for me
to wake Owu quickly.

I try.
But there is silence in his stare.

The unmoving of his limbs
and the rattling sound of death
when he does not wake
are the last things
I hear
before
we are shoved
away.

REST IN PEACE

Seeing Owu's body
lying prone
on the ground,
asleep one moment,
lifeless the next,
a boy, like me
no longer,
sends tremors
through me.

It will be okay, Auntie Afua whispers,
clasping her strong fingers
in mine
to calm
my shivering.
He is free now, Kofi.

LEAVING

REST IN PEACE

One guard leads us
with a lamp
through a hatch
in the wall
that opens
to an even darker
underground tunnel
while the other
stands at our rear
with a firestick
daring us
not to obey.

I hold on to Afua
through the narrow passageway,
which holds a haunting light
at its uncertain end
that we are pushed toward.

The crashing of water
grows so loud
the farther we walk

I worry it will somehow rush in
and devour me.

At the end
of the tunnel
is an archway of daylight
is a curved opening
is an entrance
to some unknown.

A door
of no return.

TERROR

On the other side
of the door

is the edge
of the mighty blue

that Nana Mosi
has talked about

that I have dreamed of
a body of water

so awesome
and large

it could breathe
a million clouds

drag the moon
across its gigantic waves

but this is not a dream
I am trying to climb out of

this roaring blue
is an angry nightmare

is a monstrous mouth
and it is wide enough

to swallow us
whole.

WE ARE FORCED

into a wooden boat
like the one War Horn stole us in.

Maybe they are taking us home, I say,
trying to crush the fear
with a tiny hope.
Maybe, Afua answers,
as we paddle
away from the castle door
toward a colossal vessel
sitting in the middle
of the distant sea.

FLYING HOME

A trio of large, long-tailed
white-necked birds
fly low near us
skimming for small fish
before soaring back
toward the shore.

If only.

AHEAD

of our flatboat
are dozens more
lined up
next to a massive, sand-colored
floating fort
with two masts
that fly a large, tattered banner
with seven bright red stripes
and thirty-three very white stars.

THE UNLOADING

From the distance,
I count sixty-seven
shackled men pushed and pulled,
climbing out
and up.

When it is our turn
I look back
at the world we are leaving
at the seabirds
soaring above the shore
at the tall palms
waving goodbye
and for a second
wonder
if I should dive in
and swim
for my life.

Afua smiles at me, then
shakes her head,
eyeing the giant cannon

pointing at us
from above,
whose shots
would certainly
outrace me.

A ROPE LADDER

drops down
next to our boat.

Beneath a black eagle
with stretched arms and feet

painted onto the ship's side
I make out the carved letters: USS *Georgetown.*

Standing atop is
a man as pale

and pink
as rotten coconut meat

with a shiny, golden cross
dangling

from a chain
around his neck

who yells out numbers
in the same foreign language

that Mr. Phillip insisted
we learn.

I whisper to Afua
that they are counting us.

The white gaze
of a dozen more men

greets us
as we climb up

and onto
this strange, wooden world.

To myself
I say

what I cannot pretend
is not a final goodbye

to Kwasi
to my family

to my beloved Asante.
To home.

HEAD COUNT

71, gal
72, gal
73, boy
74, boy
75, gal
76, gal
shouts a man
holding a leaflet
with a white hand,
a pipe dangling
from his hairy mouth,
before I am pushed
into a cage
on the deck
of the big boat
with Afua
and the rest.

77, boy.

TO THE WHITE FACES

with their sinister plans
and long guns
holding crooked power
and our destiny
in their thieving white hands,
we are not human.
But we are.
You must remember that,
Afua whispers,
touching my forehead
and the left side
of my chest,
no matter our fate.

DAY ONE

She whispers us
the tale of
why Anansi has eight legs
with so much emotion
that we cannot help
but feel each woe
and wonder.

Each time she introduces
a new food
that Anansi grabs
with his webs—sweet potato,
beans, honey—she licks
her lips
and rubs her belly
and we almost forget
that this big boat is moving
farther and farther away
from the castle,
that our home
is getting smaller
and smaller.

NIGHT TWO

All the bouncing
up and down
from the waves
has her sick,
so there are no stories
to pass the time,
only howls
and hollers
and songs of despair
from the men
down below
to remind us
of this slow passage
over troubled waters.

DAY THREE

Each day
at the same time
with the same scowls
and curses,
our captors
who grow filthier
and filthier
bring up the shackled men
from below
to be doused
with buckets of water,
and force them
to dance
to entertain
and even though
we cannot see their faces
from our side
of the ship,
Afua tells me to listen
very closely
to what they are singing,
that the words

have meaning,
that there is a message
in them
for us.

NIGHT SEVEN

The purple-blue sky
brings with it
a cloud of gloom
over us.

The crying is longer
and louder now.

Nana Mosi says
a purple sky means
ruin and wreckage
approaches.

Afua tries her best
to settle the women
and the boys, by humming
a soft song,
and then like a schoolteacher,
she offers to us
something very familiar:

The sun shines on those who stand up for themselves,
before it shines on those who kneel to cowardice.

CONVERSATION WITH AFUA

I have heard that before, from a man, a warrior, who
    tried to help us.
A decent man then.

He said something similar right before they killed
    him. How can there be truth to what you both
    say?
No one can kidnap your beliefs, if you believe them
    with every bone of your body. No one can shackle
    your will, Kofi.

My brother, Kwasi, was murdered too, I say, realizing
    that this is the first time I have thought of him,
    on the ship. He was planning to go to the town of
    Bonwire to study kente weaving. If he had left,
    he would still be here.
I am very sorry, Kofi.

It happened right in front of me. And they left him
    for dead. I do not want to forget him.
The healers say that Ayiye welcomes ancestors home,
    magnifies our precious memories, and brings
    peace to us.

Well, he did not get Ayiye, so there can be no peace.
Then let us have our funeral.

That is not possible.
Oh, but it is.

I do not understand.
We do not need the body to honor the spirit of a man.

. . .

Let us celebrate Kwasi, Owu, my unnamed child,
    and all the decent men, here, now.

But how?
With a praise song.

What will we say?
Let us call their memories to each other now. Then
    we will speak whatever it is that we feel, yes?

Yes.

A PRAISE SONG

for

He who is firstborn son of Addo and Efe

He who is powerful Asante birthed by Mensah

He who is noble brother with righteous heart

He who is sleek in body

He who is tall and beautiful

He who is gifted with cunning and grace

He who is magnificent doer

and cistern of bravery

lantern of wit

and clarion of joy

He who is dreamer of reds and gold

black jewel of my parents' pride.

Loud talker and joker,

best friend to all, but especially to me.

Kwasi, Brother Kwasi, how I miss you,

once river of great strength,

where you flow now

there is no end,

and this fight is not over.

This is a praise song for

He who is kindred soul
He who walks with gentle swagger
He who carries me in his arms like water
He who is protector, now humbly watching over

He who is innocent child
He who not long sprang from my loins.
Radiant son.
Though I have eyes, I am blinded
by a vision that no longer sees you

Two souls that stand guard
Where are your faces my loves?
They say that those who loved you
return to you in dreams.

Each nightfall I will look for you
climb the highest mountains
search every shadow on Earth.
Where you roam now
there are no hunters
and good deeds are the currency.
I am better because of you,
richer in purpose
and praise.

Hail to you
Owu and Two Fish
the decent men
bold like fire
your embers lighting
our way

This is a praise song
for hammerers of hope
carving a life of good
for the strong men
who will keep coming

for the departed
for the beautiful ones

For the beautiful ones yet unborn
For the beautiful ones yet unborn.

NIGHT EIGHT

I fall asleep
carrying Kwasi's face
in my heart
and wake up
with a welcome peace
of mind.

DAY ELEVEN

When the waters calm
we watch with silent curiosity
as the men with no color
fill their bottles
with brown spirits
from large barrels,
play loud, drinking games
and stumble around
like lost dogs.

On day twelve
they drop
like too-ripe fruit
and sleep
long into thirteen.

And by the twilight
of day nineteen
they have added
something new
and cruel
to their drunken ritual.

NIGHT NINETEEN

Their feet bloodied
from the broken glass
of smashed bottles,
the men with no color—the ones
who do not pass out—each drag
a girl
from our cage.

When they grab Afua
I stand up
wrap my arms around
her waist
clamp my leg
over hers
try to stop them
from taking her
to the other side
but a hard blow
to my head
knocks me down
and my arms go limp
just as the world
vanishes.

IN THIS DREAM

a flock of big, black birds
with bright red pouches
and long, wide wings
swoop down
like angels
diving from the heavens
and snatch everyone
off the ship
except me.

One of them perches
on my arm
as if it recognizes me,
then flies off.

WHEN I WAKE

Afua is next to me,
tears
            sliding
                        down
                                    her face
like rain.

She stares   up
at the purpling clouds
moving   like an angry sea   across the sky.

For days, she is quiet,
distant, like our past.

With each nightfall
a little more hope
                        sinks.

THINGS HAVE COME TO THIS

The chant and cries below
echo louder than the waves
beneath us
stronger than the wind
above.

There is a storm coming,
and its edge grows closer,
darker
than the hearts
of the men
with no color.

Every time one of them dies
from some calamity,
more brown spirits are poured,
then the grievers kneel
with heads bowed,
peeking into
their clasped hands,
mumbling
hollowed words.

When one of us dies,
there is no ceremony
no words
no nothing.
They just toss them over
for the sharks
to feast.

Death is everywhere.

At night, I count the stars
to pass the time
and each time
there are less than before.

Nana Mosi says
that stars are the eyes
of the past
watching over us.

Each day
I wonder
if I am forgotten
by Maame and Papa.

I worry if yesterday was a dream
and this nightmare
is my future.

Things have come to that.

DAY TWENTY-THREE

When Afua does speak again
it is like my maame
leaving
for the daylong trip
to the market,
and reminding me
of all the small
and big things
I must remember
to do—from chores
to cleaning my teeth—as if
she is not coming back
for a while.

STAND TALL

There is hope, Afua whispers. *The men below prepare
    to revolt.*
To revolt? How do you know this? I ask.

The song they sing, do you hear it?
Yes, it is the same, over and over.

*It is a song of flight. They have figured out how to
    unloose their chains.*
And what will they do then?

*When it is time, you will know. And you will stand
    tall, to the rising sun. Yes?*
Yes.

And you will believe in your freedom, yes?
Yes.

*It is your right, Kofi. No one can give it. No one can
    take it. It will not be easy to survive that which
    you are not meant to, but you must know your
    worth, fight to maintain it. Do not forget what
    your auntie says.*
Afua, why do you speak as if—

Agoo!
Ame.

I will die before I let them kill me again.
But you ... you will escape, I promise you.
Follow your dream.
And remember to listen
for the song ...

SONG OF FLIGHT

Escape? How?
Are we to walk
on water?

Is she telling me
that the men below
have wings?

Something Mr. Phillip
used to boast
before he gave us
his English lessons
pops into my head:
This is a new world.
There is no flying
from fate.

NIGHT TWENTY-SEVEN

Afua is not dragged out
this time,
because she does not resist.

The eager man unshackles her
and pulls her
with no trouble
from our cage.

She turns,
looks at me
with steeled eyes
as if
she is assured and ready
as if
she has the power.

When she smiles
at me, it is like
she has just seen
the next move
in a game

of Oware
and her victory
is destined.

Then she does the unimaginable.

MUTINY

While he closes
and locks the gate,
she stomps the sharp heel
of her calloused foot
into the back of his knee
with so much force
that his bone
nearly pops out
of its skin.

The popping kneecap
is a crack of lightning
to my ears.

Her violent laugh
and his painful howl
are alarms.

By the time
the drunken others come
to the rescue
with their guns hoisted

and their pink faces panicked
it is too late.

Afua has climbed
on the ship's wooden railing,
holding the wounded man's dagger
to his own neck, and
damning them all—*I curse you.*
And you. And you, she says, pointing
to our captors.
Your children will not have children.
And the sea will open up,
swallow you bone by wonderful bone,
blood and water. So be it!

She turns to me, smiles, says,
Do not forget to listen for the beautiful things, Kofi,
drops the blade,
spreads each arm out wide,
like she is holding on to the world.

Then she jumps.

AND WHAT AM I SUPPOSED TO DO

when my dreams drown?

When the door
to the last sliver of hope
is sealed?

What am I supposed to do now
in this land of cold
underneath
an arch of pallor
with no comfort
to blanket
the gloom,
to protect me
from the swallowing blues
all around us?

I NO LONGER COUNT THE DAYS

since Ama and I shared a coconut
since Ebo and I raced to the river last
since my brother's undoing
since I have seen my family
since Afua leapt overboard

or the number of tears
from the crying children beside me
or the number of times
the girls are taken
and returned
and taken
or the grumbles
from my hollowed stomach
or the falling clouds
or the thunderclaps
or the nights
of terror chasing me
or the disappearing stars.
Now I only count
the black holes left
in the graying chambers
of my breaking heart.

BATTEN DOWN

The rain, once just a hint,
a slow, single weep,
is now a full-on storm.

The purple sky pours,
the wind races
in circles,
knocking the rowdy waves
into our vessel.

And the men with no color
scatter about
distressed, hollering
trying to maneuver
the tilting ship.

WRECKED

The seventh time we slam
into the swelling sea
feels like we have hit
a massive rock.

The force of the crash
rattles the cage door open
and we are thrown
into each other,
and onto the decks.

I hear desperate cries
as some of the men
with no color
are lifted up
and overboard.

I can make out two words
that they keep screaming
over and over.

ABANDON SHIP!

THE SEA IS A RAGING MONSTER

and it has come to slay
all in its den.

The wooden ship is no match
for the nonstop battering,

the ferocious pounding.
But still it fights

to right itself
until it can no longer.

SHATTERED

THE SEA IS A
MONSTER

I miss grabbing sweet mango
on the way
to getting wood
for my maame.

I crave the red berries
that Ebo and I ate
to grow taller.

The necklace I began making
for Ama
still sits next
to my bed
atop the book
I never returned
to Mr. Phillip.

I hope that the ancestors do dwell beneath
to assist us, because
I need them now...

These are all the things
swimming

in my mind
when we crash
into what feels like
a solid wall of water
and the ship splits in half
like the shell
of a coconut.

WRATH AND FURY

Inch by inch
the ship sinks
and one by one
I watch
the same happen to
wailing boys
and girls
and for the first time
I see the big men
from below
up close
some still chained together
shouting
in familiar
and unfamiliar tongues
thrashing
and bashing
and disappearing.

I hold on
to a wedge of the ship
sliced away
in the wreck

and watch the helpless wonderfuls
crying like babies
drag each other
under.

My heart hammers away
at my chest.
I turn my eyes
in each direction
wondering which way
is somewhere
when I think
I spot
one of the long, wide, white-breasted black birds
from home,
hovering.
When it is time, you will know. Follow your dream,
I hear Afua say.

So, I do.

CLIMBING THE SKY

Like an invisible twine
the big sea wraps itself
around me
and pulls,
so I lift my shoulders
every muscle
in my arms and legs
ready to follow
ready to dance
in rhythm
to the way
of the water
ready to chase
my freedom
farther
than I have ever swum before
but just as I prepare
to dive down
and take off,
I hear,
louder than the wind

and the storming clouds
that slap the waves ...

KOFI, HELP PLEASE!

KINDRED

There, a dozen strokes away
among the floating rubble
and drowning bodies
head barely above
restless water
grasping the red-and-blue flag
teeth as white as its stars
is my cousin.

A family tie is like the river,
I can hear Nana Mosi saying,
it can bend, but it cannot break.
Is this a dream?

I grab him, look into his eyes,
and see a helpless boy
scared like me,
maybe more.

You were here, down below, I say.
His nods are shivers.

Who else? Ebo?
Daabi.

I want to ask him
about Ama
and my family
but the storm is impatient
and the lightning shooting
through the sky
shoves all thoughts
but escape
from my mind.

WE MUST GO, I scream.
But they will kill us.

Look around, they are all gone now.
But we cannot.

KOKODURU! I scream. WE CAN!
But where?

There, I say, pointing in the direction I saw the bird
    climbing the sky.
How?

We will fly.
What do you mean, chale?

And it never felt so good
to hear my cousin call me that.

In the hull of ruin,
in the midst of death,
I almost smile.

Follow me, chale, I got you!
I say to him,
right before
I spread my wings
and soar
into the purpled
unknown.

So, he does,
paddling,
kicking,
mirroring
my every move.

And together, we fly.

ACKNOWLEDGMENTS

Black history began way before 1619. It didn't start on the banks of the James River in Jamestown, Virginia, or in dilapidated cabins clustered on the Monticello plantation. Africa was our genesis. I knew this from first grade, maybe even before that... You see, my parents read to me books like *Moja Means One, And the Sun God Said: That's Hip*, and *Mufaro's Beautiful Daughters*...made me memorize poems like "Heritage" by Countee Cullen and "Ego-Tripping" by Nikki Giovanni...filled my adolescent bookshelves with novels like *Two Thousand Seasons* and *Things Fall Apart*...and told me stories and folktales that introduced me to Anansi the Spider, ancient Egypt, Queen Nzinga, Mount Kilimanjaro, and the Golden Stool of the Asante Kingdom long before I sat (on one of the five wooden replica Asante stools in our home) glued to our black-and-white television night after night watching *Roots*, the saga of an American family. So first I want to thank Mom and Dad, for showing me that while the brutal captivity and bondage of Africans was a part of my story, it was not the first chapter, or even the second . . . What a gift they gave me.

Every story has a beginning, a middle, and an end. I wrote this one because people need to know that the middle was not our beginning. I wanted to speak the truth about the history of African Americans, because while most of us are aware of the *American* part, it's time for us to know more about the *African* part, right?

I first visited Africa in 2012. Juanita Britton, a businesswoman and mentor, became the Queen Mother of a village in the Eastern Region of Ghana, and she invited me to her coronation ceremony. It was here where I walked along the beaches and through the markets, rediscovering the land of my mother's mothers with my sisters and brothers: David, Tracy, Renee, Jessica, Lindsay, Goldie, Ed, Kenny, and Kim. It was here where I met friends that felt like long-lost family: Emefa, Elvis, Larbi, Mr. Easy, Daniel, and Lady Delphine. Eleven times I have returned, eaten my fair share of jollof rice and tilapia, danced to many a drummer's beat, listened to countless elders' stories, attended church and a funeral, built a library in a rural village, and cried each time I visited Elmina Castle and Cape Coast Castle: the complex, sinister, and heartbreaking holding places for Africans captured during the transatlantic trafficking and trade of human beings. Over the years, my soul has looked back on these impactful journeys, knowing that one day they would find their way into a book...Thank you, Juanita, for making this possible.

I thought about this book for three years before I wrote a word. When I finally sat down to compose it, there were many pauses and breaks in the creative process. I am a hopeful person, full of fiery optimism. But I knew this would be a toilsome tale to tell... And it was, full of heartache. It is only because I had people around me offering encouragement, feedback, and comfort that I was able to finish. I am grateful to my agent, business partner, and matchless dreamer Arielle Eckstut, the one true literary genius I know. My resourceful and loyal writing assistant, Cass. My allies, best friends, and creative inspirers, Randy, Mary, and Angel. Deneen Howell and Bob Barnett, lawyers with unparalleled diplomacy and bookish sagacity. The American School in London for the residency that afforded me an abundance of time and creative space to dive into this big sea. My supportive former publishing colleagues, Ellen, Cat, Mary, John, and Lisa. Jackie and Jason, for your wisdom and writerly kinship. Nana Brew-Hammond, Tinesha Davis, Alice Cardini, Ann Marie Stephens, and Michael V.

Williams, for reading early drafts and offering a critical and compassionate eye, and Beatrice Amorkor Saba for the countless stories about growing up in Ghana she shared over fried plantain and Red Red and for her abounding insight and trueheartedness.

I have been in this business for most of my life, from working for my father's publishing company as a child to running a small press after college to building a career in children's literature, and I like to think I can recognize publishing professionals who employ equal parts vision and smarts . . . Little, Brown Books for Young Readers is home to such people, and I am thankful to be a guest in your house: Margaret Raymo, my near decades-long editor and masterly literary conductor, I appreciate you. Megan Tingley and Michael Pietsch, I appreciate your faith. Victoria, Sydney, Shawn, Marisa, Emilie, Christie, Hannah, and Jen, I appreciate everything you've done and will do to share this story with the world.

The Door of No Return is the saga of an African family. I could not have written it if it weren't for the love and support and strength of my own: Stephanie, your thoughts and suggestions and ideas and soul are all over this book, as they are with everything I've ever written, so this is as much your story as it is mine: Medase. Nandi, you have been the progenitor of my creativity since my first book, and whether near or far, that will always be...There's an African proverb that says, *We desire to bequeath two things to our children; the first one is roots, the other one is wings.* Samayah, for all the weeks I was away at a writer's retreat figuring this story out, or the days I was sequestered in my studio writing, or the nights I couldn't play cards because I was rewriting, I can only hope that this story was worth it, that it has wings. Because I wrote it for you, and your friends, and their friends. So y'all can fly.

Kwame Alexander
London, England
January 2022

TWI GLOSSARY

Twi is one of two languages (the other is Fante) of the Akan, a large ethnic group inhabiting southern Ghana. The Asante people are a part of the Akan, and they speak Twi. The Twi alphabet is made up of twenty-two letters. Out of these, twenty are found in the twenty-six-lettered English alphabet. The two letters Ɛɛ and Ɔɔ are the only ones that you'll find in Twi but not in English. There are some words that use these two letters that I've modified for pronunciation.

Aboa means "animal" or "beast."

Agoo means to "pay attention" or "Do you hear me?" The response is always **Ame**, which means you are "willing to listen" or "Yeah, I hear you!" The literal translation is to "build together."

Akwaaba means "welcome," as in to greet someone when they arrive at your house or in your country.

Ayiye means "funeral."

The literal translation of **Bayere** is "yam." I chose it as the name of the Kings Festival because the people of Kwanta are celebrating the harvest of the yam.

The **Benda** is a historical unit of weight of the Asante people for measuring gold dust.

Chale is a popular term of endearment used when addressing a friend, like "What's up, *bro*?" or "*Girl*, don't be late!"

Chay chay koo-lay is the pronunciation of a Ghanaian children's song, "Kye Kye Kule." My mother used to sing it with me and my siblings when we were kids.

Cowrie shells were used for centuries as currency in Africa.

Daabi means "no."

Dondo is the hourglass-shaped talking drum that is played while held under the arm. It has other names in different regions of Africa. For example, it's called the tama in the country of Senegal. Another drum played in Ghana is the dundun.

Dunwõtwe is the number eighteen. The actual Twi spelling is *dunwɔtwe*.

Ei is pronounced *ey* and connotes the utterance "eh" or "whoa," depending on the context.

Ekutu means "orange," as in the fruit. But it's not Twi. It's actually a word spoken in the Fante language, which is from the Fante people, who are prominent on the coast of Ghana.

Ete sen is a traditional greeting for when you first see someone. It means "How are you?" The actual Twi spelling is *Ɛte sɛn*.

Kenkey is a West African dish similar to dumplings, usually served with pepper sauce and fried fish or soup.

Kente is a type of silk and cotton fabric made of colorful, interwoven cloth strips. Formerly only worn by royalty, kente cloth is worn today by many people, who regard it as a symbol of African pride and dignity.

Kokoduru is my abbreviation of the phrase *koko yε duru*, which means "to be brave." I use it here as a way of declaring "I got this" or "You got this."

Komm means "quiet" or "silence."

Maame is "mother" or "mommy."

Medase means "Thank you."

Me din de means "My name is" and is used to introduce yourself.

Me ko is spelled *Me kɔ* and means "I go" or "I gotta go" or, as I understand it, "I'm outta here."

Nana is a gender-neutral title representing the highest office in society. It is also a term used to denote "grandmother," "grandfather," or "elder."

Ose yie is an Asante war chant I found on one of the great crooner/activist Harry Belafonte's old albums.

Red Red is a Ghanaian dish (like Kofi, my absolute, hands-down favorite) comprised of black-eyed peas. The dish derives its name from the color it takes on from the red palm oil in which it's cooked (and the fried plantain sometimes served with it).

Wahala means "trouble."

Ye ko is spelled *Ye kɔ* and means "Let's go" or "We go" or, as I sometimes say, "We're outta here."

ADINKRA SYMBOLS
(In Order of Appearance)

I placed these symbols at the beginning of each section to foreshadow what's about to happen. Used for hundreds of years by Ghanaians, Adinkra symbols capture the history, way of life, and philosophy of the Asante people. Their representations and meanings are linked to fables and are used to bestow wisdom and knowledge. They are popular on fabrics, pottery, buildings, and crafts and as tattoos.

Sankofa is portrayed by a mythical bird turning its head backward to eat a precious egg. The symbol means that we should remember and learn from the past to make positive progress in the future. The literal translation is "to retrieve."

Mpatapo represents the bond or knot that binds parties in a dispute to a peaceful, harmonious reconciliation. It is a symbol of peacemaking after strife.

Bese Saka is the symbol of power, abundance, plenty, togetherness, and unity. It also symbolizes agriculture and trade. The literal translation is "a sack of cola nuts."

Funtunfunefu-Denkyemfunefu depicts two joined crocodiles and represents cooperation and democracy. The crocodiles share one stomach, yet they fight over food. This popular symbol is a reminder that infighting and tribalism is harmful to all who engage in it.

Nkyinkyim represents the idea that life's journey is a twisted, often tortuous journey requiring resilience and versatility. The literal translation is "twisted."

Epa symbolizes bondage, captivity, law, and justice. The literal translation is "handcuffs," which were introduced in Africa by European invaders and later became popular among chiefs in cuffing offenders of the law.

Aya is a symbol of endurance and resourcefulness represented by the fern. The fern is a hardy plant that can grow in inhospitable places. An individual who wears the Aya symbol has endured many adversities and outlasted much difficulty.

Bin Nka Bi represents peace and harmony. It depicts two fish biting each other's tails, and the direct translation is "No one should bite the other." Although the symbol doesn't appear before a section in the book, I include it here because it is the tattoo on the side of Two Fish's face.

LOCATIONS USED IN
THE DOOR OF NO RETURN

Akra, also known as Accra, is the largest city in Ghana. It became the capital in 1877 and sits right on the coast of the Gulf of Guinea, which feeds into the Atlantic Ocean.

Bonwire is a town in Ghana, where the most popular cloth in Africa, known as kente, originated.

Cape Coast is the capital of the Central Region of Ghana. It too sits on the Gulf of Guinea. In the seventeenth century, the Swedish built the Cape Coast Castle that was later used by the British as a holding prison for kidnapped Africans.

Kumasi is the capital of the Asante Region in southern Ghana. It is celebrated as the center of Asante culture with its Kejetia Market and the National Cultural Center.

Offin River is a waterway in Ghana. It is located in the Tano-Offin Forest Reserve, which is in Ghana's Atwima Mponua District. It has steep channels and an average depth of twelve to fifteen meters.

Pra River is the largest river out of the three principal rivers in Ghana, with a length of 149 miles.

Upper Kwanta and **Lower Kwanta** are places that I imagined, based on real places that I've been to, or read about, in Ghana.